SILENCE
IN THE
GARDEN

SILENCE
IN THE
GARDEN

A NOVEL

JC CRUMPTON

SHANNON
OGHMA CREATIVE MEDIA
www.oghmacreative.com

Copyright © 2017 by JC Crumpton

All rights reserved. No part of this book may be reproduced in any form without the express written permission of the publisher.

The characters and events in this book are fictitious. Any similarity to real persons, living or dead, is entirely coincidental and not intended by the author.

ISBN: 978-1-63373-284-1

Interior Design by Casey W. Cowan
Editing by Gordon Bonnet

Shannon Press
Oghma Creative Media
Bentonville, Arkansas
www.oghmacreative.com

For my parents,
who taught me to love a good story.

ACKNOWLEDGEMENTS

The first hints of this book originated long ago during trips with the PTMC to Eureka Springs where we would sit on a rock wall and look across the valley at the Crescent Hotel. She towered above us in reality as well as the imagination and something stirred. So from the beginning, a lot of people deserve a shout out for helping in some shape or form along the way.

A special thank is needed for my editor Gordon Bonnett, a fine writer in his own right. His insightful input added so much more to the story. J.H. Fleming also warrants much gratitude. She volunteered to read an advance copy and pointed out those little errors that always seem to be missed even in the fourth and fifth read-through of the manuscript.

There are others that deserve a high-five, a rousing cheer, and a slap on the back: the staff of Oghma Creative Media (especially because their work is never done), Richard Howk, Venessa Cerasale, Olga Berg, Joan Lisle, Brenda Hyslip, and all the other intrepid members of the critique group Authors Anonymous.

I want to thank my parents, teachers, professors, friends, and family that instilled in me a love for telling tall tales. Most of all, I want to thank my wonderful and beautiful wife Chrissi for letting me hide away at nights and weekends to complete this story, and my children Edan and Hayley who try not to roll their eyes when I think of new things to add.

WEDNESDAY, NOVEMBER 12, 2003

"He who was living is now dead / We who were living are now dying."
—T.S. Eliot, *"The Waste Land."*

Not even the stories of ghosts and rumors of strange tragedies could keep her away. It took years to plan the trip to Eureka Springs but only moments—in comparison—to execute. The remnants of a Wednesday morning rush hour in Dallas had cleared by the time Shari pulled her two-door, blue Camry out onto the road at nine o'clock. Her driveway quickly faded away in her review mirror. After suffering through the expansive fields of dry grass in Eastern Oklahoma, the sight of hills and thick forests as she turned north on I-540 broke the monotony, making the drive more memorable. With every corner she rounded and rise she topped, she found herself holding her breath, her imagination captivated by the Ozark Mountains. The area had experienced a wet summer and presented itself with autumn colors of fiery red and orange. The spaces between the trees that crept to the edges of the road hid moist shadows the late afternoon sun couldn't seem to penetrate.

She didn't know why she had waited this many years before taking the trip—but an emergency at work that kept her home two years ago had ruined previously set reservations. When she saw the old Victorian inn towering above her at the end of Crescent Drive, she knew why this rustic little town attracted so many visitors from all over the world. The Crescent Hotel looked down on Eureka Springs from the crest of West Mountain like an old matriarch keeping a careful eye on her children. Her Granny Millie had told her long ago that it had been built back in 1886 and had remained a constant symbol of a bygone era through the turmoil of depression, the ups and downs of tourism, and the depredations of the modern world that seemed to care not a whit for history.

After leaving her car in the parking lot, Shari stepped through glass doors bordered and edged with aged brass that glowed with a muted brilliance, as if the years had sapped away some of its luster. Nineteen years ago, she had promised to fulfill her great-grandmother's dying wish—to return something that had been removed almost a century ago.

The lobby opened into a broad room lit by two aged chandeliers, and looking out over a terraced garden, windows rose from the floor to the top of the ceiling almost twenty feet above her head. A thick, white brick fireplace to her right—its hearth open on both sides—filled most of the sitting area across from the front desk. The counter and two high-backed settees in front of the fireplace took up the front half of the lobby. Shari turned to the left and stepped up to what looked to her like one of those old-fashioned teller windows she had seen in banks on countless western movies.

While she waited for the desk clerk to take care of the customer in front of her, Shari half-listened to a tall, thin man dressed in gray pants and a single-breasted wool coat as he spoke with whom she assumed was the hotel manager. The businessman—and the suit made Shari believe this—stood in front of the concierge desk a few steps from the counter toward the back wall. The man's coat hung off his shoulders loosely enough for it to look a bit oversized but still trendy. Sitting behind the concierge desk, the manager nodded several times and never took his eyes off the man in gray.

"Have you ever heard of the television show *Paranormal Inquiry*?" The tall man pulled a business card out of his pocket and handed it to the manager. "We have looked into the legends surrounding the Crescent Hotel and feel that this represents a great opportunity for both your establishment as well as our program."

The manager held the card in his right hand and flicked the edges of it with his left forefinger. "I will have to talk to the owners, but I don't see why they wouldn't be interested in something like this."

"Good. Have their lawyers contact us, and we can arrange a meeting to go over the details. They can call the number on the card."

Shari stared at the two men and didn't realize the customer in front of her had finished until he mumbled an apology as he tried to carry his bags away. It didn't take long for the clerk to assign her a room, passing her the key with a smile. The young man, who couldn't have been long out of high school, pointed beyond the fireplace toward the elevator on the other side of the lobby. She followed the well-trod wood floors past the lounge area with its carpet patterned with raised geometric designs.

A fat orange tabby sat in the overstuffed chair on the back side of the fireplace. It ignored Shari when she walked to the elevator, content to sleep with its paws tucked under its body. A framed picture of what looked to be the same cat hung beside the elevator, and Shari skimmed the words after pushing the call button. Apparently, the cat napping in the chair was the fourth generation of orange tabbies to reside at the hotel.

The elevator opened, and she stepped into the car, selecting the button for the third floor, and just as the doors were creaking closed, a young boy stuck his hand between them and started screaming as if the doors had cut off his hand. The doors slid back open and the boy jumped into the car. A girl with loose strawberry blonde curls looking just a little younger than the boy stepped into the elevator and slugged him lightly in the arm.

"Don't do that, Chase." She furrowed her brows into a tight frown and pursed her lips. "You know that scares me every time you do that, and Mother even said you're not to do it."

The boy shrugged. "So?" He turned to the elevator console and started to select all the buttons, but his mother came in and swatted his hand away before he could.

"Chase, you know better than to push all the buttons when there are the people in the elevator." The woman held her hand against the door while her husband, carrying a large duffel over one shoulder and wheeling a large suitcase, came in behind her. She looked at Shari. "Sorry. They get excited whenever we travel."

Shari shrugged. "I used to be the same way at their age."

"Was that a long time ago?" The boy smiled.

"Chase."

He looked at his mother. "What?"

Setting the duffel bag on the floor of the elevator car, the father lowered his head at his son. "Chase. It's not polite to say things about a lady's age."

Shari brushed it off with a wave of her hand. "No problem. He didn't mean anything by it."

The man lifted one corner of his mouth in a lopsided grin. "Still. Chase," he insisted.

Chase bowed his and head and shuffled his feet. "Sorry."

"No harm," Shari said.

The elevator doors ground closed, and the car began its ascent. Stuck back in the corner, the father pulled out a brochure and began to flip through the panels. The two children continued their bickering, arguing about who would get the remote control and what program they would watch once they reached the room. Smiling in a tight-lipped grin, the mother shook her head.

"Hmm." The father grunted and looked up from his phone. Shari and the woman both looked at him. He nodded toward the papers and advertisements pinned behind a glass door on the elevator walls.

"What is it, babe?" the woman asked.

"It seems this place has a history of being haunted." He widened his eyes at Chase and grinned.

The boy reached over and grabbed his sister with both hands. "Oooh," he wailed, and the sound caused Shari to wince.

"Chase." His mother grabbed his hands when he started to reach for his sister. "Say sorry for hurting that poor woman's ears."

"It's all right. I guess it's payback for all the years I was loud."

The woman frowned, and then shrugged. "Still. It hurts my ears too."

Little Chase, a wide grin stretching across his face, stepped closer to Shari and looked up at her. "My daddy and I are going to find one of the ghosts." He looked over his shoulder at his father. "Ain't we, Daddy?"

The father smiled. "Sure, son. Maybe right after the train ride."

"A train?" Chase shrieked. The boy turned his head back to Shari and pushed against his father's legs, his attention quickly changing to something different. His father put his hand on the boy's head and tousled his hair.

Shari smiled and watched as Chase tried to push his way between his sister and the front of the elevator. As soon as the door opened on the third floor, the two children took off squealing down the hall, their earlier argument forgotten.

When Shari reached her room, she put the key card in the slot and pushed the door open with her hip. The sudden scent of soft must and old powder nearly overwhelmed her. It reminded her of her youth—a comforting fragrance that made her think of those afternoon trips up to Tulsa to see her grandparents. It reminded her of their three-story Victorian house with dimly-lit halls and shadowed staircases. An easy smile came to her lips, and she suddenly wanted to play tag through the halls while grown-ups talked about boring things over steaming cups of coffee in the kitchen.

Stairs led to the penthouse on the other side of the door, and after climbing the steps, Shari tossed her overnight bag onto the bed. She sat at the vanity in the room, looking in the mirror and rubbing the bridge of her nose between her thumb and forefinger for a few seconds. A headache had started to creep in and take up permanent residence behind her forehead toward the end of her seven-hour drive. She rummaged through her makeup bag for a bottle of Motrin and rolled two pills out into the palm of her hand. A quick swallow of water washed them down, and she stood up to begin unpacking.

She put her clothes in the wardrobe. Pulling back the quilted comforter, she lay down on the bed and closed her eyes. The thought that she might be lying in the very same room her great-grandmother had stayed in while enrolled at the Crescent College and Conservatory for Young Women back in the early 1920s made her smile and start to relax.

Long drives always made her anxious, and she had continuously tried not to think about everything that could go wrong but couldn't prevent it no matter how hard she tried. Ever since high school if she could worry about it, she would, often giving herself an evening with an upset stomach or headache. The fact that she had made the drive to Eureka Springs by herself made her feel like she had accomplished something. When she tried to make the trip a couple years back, it didn't take much of an emergency for her to cancel her plans. This time she stepped way out of her comfort zone and made the journey. Now nothing could prevent her from completing the task her Granny Millie had asked her to do.

"Promise me you will take it back, Shari Anne," Granny Millie had said almost twenty years ago.

"But you have worn it for so long." Shari remembered how she had run her fingers over the gold locket and its finely-wrought chain. The same shape she had seen in the weathervane atop the hotel.

Granny Millie shook her head, holding Shari's hands in her own. Her palms felt soft and supple, not wrinkled and cracked like the backs with their distended veins and swollen knuckles. "It never was mine. It doesn't belong to any of us. I was only supposed to hold on to it for a little while. That time has almost passed now, and it is time to pass it to the next guardian."

She looked at Shari then—not with the carefree smile in her eyes that she usually had with all of her grandchildren and great-grandchildren, but with concern and seriousness. Her hands gripped Shari's tighter. "You must do this. I won't ask you to promise. Just do it for me if you say will, but if you can't, don't do it."

Swallowing and with her heart suddenly pounding like a hammer inside her chest, Shari nodded quickly. "I will, Granny Millie. I will."

"Okay." Her great-grandmother had cupped her cheek with one hand while she put the crescent moon locket into her hands with the other. "Thank you, child."

Shari's breath slowed and her chest rose and fell evenly as she drifted off to sleep. She dreamt of the hotel as it must have been back when her Granny Millie had attended the boarding school. The 1920s, a decade of excitement and growth before the Great Depression repressed it all.

Girls of all ages walked down the halls from class to class, their white Peter Thompson dresses with long pleats and high waists swishing as they moved. Some sat in the high-backed chairs in front of the brick fireplace, filling the lobby with talk about their classes or friends, occasionally adding how much they missed their homes. Only a few of the young students didn't carry books or tablets in their arms or have them resting on the sofa cushions beside them.

Shari woke from her nap an hour later rested and energized. She got up and smoothed her hair in the mirror, making sure her makeup hadn't smeared. Reaching into a smaller bag sitting on the left side of the vanity, she pulled out the gold quarter-moon-shaped locket her Granny Millie had charged her with returning. She clasped it around her neck, taking a quick look in the mirror to watch it glint in the light against her chest.

She swiveled on the seat but jerked her head back around. The edges of the mirror had started to blacken, blocking out the reflection as if she had been retreating down a tunnel. But when she looked back, she saw nothing other than her own eyes looking back at her. Against her chest, the locket grew warmer against her skin. Then the image in the mirror beyond her own reflection blurred and began to fade to gray. She blinked her eyes rapidly and shook her head. Everything returned to normal. The trip must have worn her out more than she originally believed. But she held the locket in her fingertips, and it was no longer warm as it had been just seconds earlier. A brief shiver coursed through her body.

Ghost stories. She smiled weakly. Had the nap helped, or had it only made her realize how much fatigue ached her body and cobwebs filled her thinking? Dinner and a little nightcap might help.

She pulled the door to the north penthouse closed behind her and jiggled the handle to make sure the door had locked. As she stepped away from the door, a faint scream drifted down the hall, and the skin on back of her neck twitched. It floated to her in the still air, so soft that it could have come from the outside. Could it have been one of the kids from the elevator?

Hurrying around the corner, she sprinted down the gray-carpeted hall to the window at the far end of the wing. Only a few cars—silent but anxious metal beasts of burden—waiting for the drivers rested in the otherwise empty west parking lot.

As she turned away from the window and wondered what the sound could have been, the light fluttered in the corner of her eye. She jerked her head around. A dark shadow slipped past the end of the hall. Sprinting past several rooms, she stopped with her hand on the wall and pushed her head forward to peer around the corner.

Nothing stirred in the empty hall. She walked back up the corridor past Dr. Baker's Lounge to the elevator. A cool breeze slid across her when the doors opened, and she shivered, stepping quickly into the elevator. All the talk and mention of ghosts and spirits already had her spooked. She always professed a disbelief in ghosts and the like, preferring to think that some rational explanation existed to explain away the inexplicable events surrounding places like this old hotel. Granny Millie never believed in ghosts, but she always warned her that things worse than wailing spirits and displaced souls wandered the world.

Whenever she started in on those dire warnings, Shari's mother would just smile and stroke the back of the old woman's hand.

During the ride down to the ground floor, she looked at the different flyers on the walls and read an abbreviated history of the hotel. She found the only mention of the school in a brief paragraph that said little about the many girls that had spent years of their childhood traipsing up and down the halls. She smiled at the mention of the ghost tours offered every weekend for a nominal price. Tales of haunting and apparitions took up the majority of the flyers, leaving little space for those tourists like Shari that had a more historical interest in the hotel. What a pity for the trivial paranormal to take precedence over something as substantial and real as the Crescent Hotel's history as the home of a women's college. Especially considering the fact it occurred during the years that women had argued for and finally won the right to have their voices counted.

Anything for the almighty dollar.

If she hadn't already made plans to spend the weekend with her parents in Tulsa, she might have been tempted to take the tour just to say she had. She smiled, and the elevator settled to a stop.

After walking out of the elevator, she headed past the front counter and concierge desk to the Crystal Dining Room for dinner. A muffled, thumping rhythm from her sandals striking the wood floors followed her. Choosing the table furthest from the door and settling in, she ordered a glass of Pinot Grigio before looking around at the decor. Did the management select the antiques that littered the room in an attempt to recapture the Victorian feel? Or was it just less expensive than buying modern furniture and decorations? Everything had an aged look to it, but some of the pieces seemed less than authentic and gave her the impression that they might have been modern reproductions instead of being the genuine articles.

Quickly glancing over the menu, she decided on the Marinated Grilled South Texas Quail, wondering how good the hotel chef could render some of her home cooking. Back in Dallas, Y.O. Ranch Steakhouse had the best quail, so she wouldn't hold it against the chef if he couldn't match it. She ordered after the server returned with her wine and then tried to guess what the room had been while the school had operated—perhaps a ballroom or music conservatory.

Seated a couple of tables away from her the man in the gray suit she had seen visiting with the hotel manager sipped a red wine while his gaze drifted around the room, settling on one painting for a moment before moving on to another or a piece of furniture. He caught Shari looking at him, and before she could turn away, the man nodded and lifted his glass. She smiled back, wondering if the man's gesture had been one of politeness or actual interest. His chair grated across the wood floor as he pushed it back and stood with the glass still in his hand.

The muscle in her jaw tightened as she clenched her teeth and groaned inwardly, hoping that her annoyance at herself didn't show on her face. She looked up at the man when he stood on the other side of her table, blinking a couple of times. He was taller than she had first thought, and way too skinny. His black hair was trimmed evenly, as if he had had it done that same morning before stepping onto the plane or whatever mode of transportation he had taken to get to this remote corner of Arkansas.

"I wonder if I could ask you a quick question?" He set his glass on the table and reached his right hand toward her. "Michael Bennett."

She shook the man's hand but pulled out of his grip before he had been ready to release it. "Shari Wheatley. How can I help you, Mr. Bennett?"

He grinned, revealing straight, gleaming white teeth. "Please, call me Michael."

"Michael." She nodded once.

"I just wanted to know if you have heard anything about the legends surrounding this hotel?"

"Of course."

He raised his eyebrows. "Oh, really? And do you think any of them are true?"

She shrugged. "Could be. I've never been here before. My family's from Tulsa, Oklahoma, but I live and work in Dallas."

"I flew into Tulsa from Los Angeles." He motioned to the empty chair across from her. "May I join you?"

She waved at the chair. "For a little while. I hadn't really expected to entertain anyone for dinner."

"Just for a second." He flashed his perfect teeth at her. "I flew out from Los Angeles to find out if the hotel wanted to be part of the television program *Paranormal Inquiry*."

He paused, staring at Shari. She imagined he expected her to swoon or gawk in some awestruck manner. "Okay."

His eyes blinked several times before he finally spoke. "It is a show that tries to either prove or debunk regional legends of the paranormal variety."

"I've seen parts of the show." She took another quick swallow of her wine. "I know what it is. I'm just not that interested in it. But, please, have a seat."

"Thank you." Her rebuttal didn't seem to faze him, and he sat down in the chair after pulling it out. "I'm a producer for the show."

"I figured as much."

His lips tightened, and his left brow twitched. "How?"

"I overheard part of your conversation with the hotel manager."

"Ah." Michael grunted and grabbed the stem of his wine glass. He rubbed the back of his left hand with his right.

Before he could say anything more, Shari leveled her gaze at him. "What about this little burg and its history intrigued your studio?"

"That's the interesting part." He pushed back from the table and crossed his legs. "One of our show's creators worked on a series several years back with a young man that had graduated from one of the rural schools out here."

"From Eureka Springs?"

Michael shook his head. "Not from this town but one of the others near here, I believe."

"Okay."

"Well, it seems that they were talking over a drink after shooting had ended for the day and the subject of ghosts came up."

"Sounds odd, but okay." She lifted her glass to her lips and let the sweet flavor wash over her.

"Yeah," he said. "And it seems like he told Robert that this Crescent Hotel, once a destination place for lots of the rich and famous in the past, was just littered with ghosts and apparitions."

"Hasn't your show been on for a few years?"

"Sure." He nodded, reaching for his wine. "But it took a while to convince the studio that there was anything out here that our audience would find interesting."

"Because it's not a former prison or mental hospital where residents were tortured and used in terrible government experiments?"

Opening his mouth wide, Michael barked out a quick sharp laugh. "You may know more about our show than you let on, Miss Wheatley."

She waved her hand around in the air. "You guys advertise heavily. I've seen some of the teasers and ads."

He scooted the chair closer and leaned his elbows on the table. "But you're right. Now I'm here to see if there's anything to all these tales. It seems that the hotel has made a bit of money out of their history and possible ghosts in residence."

The young man's brow knitted. "And how is it that *you* know about these ghost tales?"

"My great-grandmother went to school here when it was the Crescent College and Conservatory for Young Women."

"And she told you all about the ghosts?"

Shari shook her head. "Goodness, no. Granny Millie didn't believe in ghosts."

Putting his chin on top of his hands, Michael watched her intently. "But do you believe in them, Miss Wheatley?"

"Nope. Can't say that I do."

"Haven't you ever seen something you couldn't explain?"

"Oh, plenty of times." Shari hoped admitting there were things for which she had no answer for didn't make her seem foolish. "I just don't believe that they've been caused by displaced spirits or disembodied souls."

"Then do you just write them off?"

"No. Just because I don't have an explanation doesn't mean there isn't one or that the phenomenon involves ghosts or anything to do with the paranormal."

"What do think it is then?"

"Probably something rare that I've never heard about."

"Like what?"

Shari leaned back in her chair and looked up at the paneled ceiling above her, thinking back to her childhood. When she had still been in high school, she had taken a summer trip with her family to Louisiana. That was one trip she did not want to experience a second time.

She looked back at Michael. "Okay. One summer, my sister and I were traveling with our parents through southern Louisiana. Swampy area. Huge cypress trees covered with curtains of Spanish moss. Real spooky."

"I can imagine." The producer nodded and kept his gaze leveled at her.

"Well we both saw this ball of greenish light bobbing through the trees. We thought it was a ghost or something like that. But later in college, I learned about methane and swamp gas, things like anaerobic decomposition."

"I always thought they were called will-o'-the-wisps and were supposed to be the spirits of evil men." The corner of his mouth crept up in a lopsided grin.

"Nope. Just rot." Shari laughed. "I guess that could be akin to evil men."

He rapped his knuckles on the table three times and sat back. "How true you are." He stood up and grabbed his wine. "I will leave you to your dinner. Thank you for your conversation."

"Thank you, Michael," she said. "If I see that you have done an episode on the Crescent Hotel, I promise that I will watch it this time."

Bending at the waist, the man bowed and then walked back to his own table. After a few minutes, he stood up and walked by Shari's table as he left. "If you get dessert, make sure you get the three-berry cobbler. Best dessert I have ever had the privilege of eating."

"I will." She waved at him. "Enjoy your stay."

He nodded and left the restaurant, heading back to the front of the hotel.

Ten minutes and a second glass of wine later, the waiter set the quail in front of her and asked her if he could get her anything else. She shook her head and smiled. The chef had marinated the quail in herbs and had laid it on a bed of rice almondine. She savored each bite as the meat slid off the bone, sipping from her wine occasionally and concentrating on her meal. It had the perfect blend of onion and lemon bitterness with the syrupy sweetness of roasted garlic.

When she couldn't find the waiter right away, she pushed her chair back and left enough money on the table for her meal and a tip. As she passed the double-sided fireplace, she saw a tall, thin man in a single-breasted brown suit and a derby of the same color waiting for the elevator. The cat had left his comfortable spot on the overstuffed chair. Someone milled about behind the counter in the gift shop across from the elevator, but she and the man were the only two people in the lobby. The front counter had a sign hanging over the glass panel—"Please ring bell for service." She smiled as the elderly man stepped out of the way and followed her into the elevator when the door slid open with its usual groan.

On the ride up, she tried to avoid the man's glance, but he stared at her with his deep-set, brown eyes. She felt his gaze on her and could smell a trace of mint. Still feeling on edge from the scream she had heard earlier and the man's constant study, the ride up to third floor took much longer in her mind than it had earlier in the day—even with the added torture of the two rowdy children. Her heart sped in her chest, its cadence pulsing in her ears.

Braving a sideways glance, she saw the man still smiling at her. She grinned and looked away. Her mouth felt dry, and she licked her lips to try to generate some moisture. When the doors moaned open, she hurried off and walked down the hall and turned into Dr. Baker's Lounge. The silver door handle tingled cool to the touch as she twisted the knob. Through the glass panes, she could see a young, slender woman with straight black hair that fell to the middle of her back standing behind the bar to the left of the entrance.

The bartender looked up as Shari came into the room. "Good evening."

"Hi." She looked around the room.

Eight wooden tables lined the walls—four on each side—surrounded by cane-backed chairs and covered with white tablecloths long enough to almost reach the floor. Two benches with burgundy cushions rested against the wall on either side of the glass door that opened onto a balcony. A black wrought-iron fence edged the terrace overlooking the town and all of its Victorian homes and narrow, twisting streets and specialty gift shops—which were only visible as rows of soft, orange and yellow lights, blurred by the leaves and branches that partially hid most of the houses.

Shari chose the table closest to the arched door and sat with her back to the balcony. She looked up when she heard the door to the bar open. The elderly man came in and, after smiling at the bartender, ordered a glass of ice water. He looked to each corner of the lounge before his gaze rested on Shari. An uncle on her mother's side of the family had retired last year from the Tulsa Police Department, and she could hear his voice in her head now—always clear the corners.

He shuffled over to her table with small, carefully-placed steps. "May I sit with you?" His voice reminded Shari of her grandfather's—quiet but gravelly, like a smoothly-idling motor.

She looked up at the man and shrugged. "Not too many people here tonight," she said. Other than the bartender, they were alone in the room. And there had only been a couple of other diners in the restaurant for dinner with her.

"Thank you." The man reached out a shaking hand and pulled the chair across from her. "Wednesday is not the busiest night around here anymore."

He sighed as he sat down, unbuttoning his jacket and smoothing the fabric that bunched up in a roll at his waist. The bartender came over and set the water in front of the man and smiled without looking over at him. She waited as Shari looked through the beverage menu.

"I'll take a glass of chardonnay," Shari requested.

"Can do," the bartender replied and headed back to the bar. Her steps stuttered, and she reached out to catch herself on the next table.

"Are you all right?" Shari pushed her chair back to stand, but the woman waved her away.

"I'm fine." She nodded and walked behind the bar.

Shari turned back to the table and watched as the man straightened his thin black tie and then looked up at Shari, catching her watching him. He smiled and raised his right eyebrow. His demeanor made her feel comfortable and at ease.

"Where are you from?"

Shari put her right fist over her mouth and cleared her throat before answering, "Dallas—Richardson actually. You?"

He smiled and ran his hand over his smooth cheeks. The bartender picked up a bottle and wrapped it in a white cloth.

"I'm a local boy, really," he replied. "Kenneth Baxter. Retired from the Eureka Springs police department over twenty years ago now."

She nodded and gripped his outstretched hand. "Shari Wheatley."

"What brought you to our Little Switzerland, Miss Wheatley?" He let her hand go, and she pulled it to her chest.

Shari chuckled. "I can see why it's called that. All the streets are crooked, and the houses are built right up against them." She nodded to the bartender when the woman set the glass of chardonnay in front of her. "It's a quaint little town."

The man met her gaze, his silence urging her to continue. She thought back to a brochure she had once read about the town. "Is it true that it's the only town in the U.S. that doesn't have any land flat enough for a rodeo ground or a football field?"

"I don't know about all the other states." He looked up at the brim of his hat and then pulled it off, setting in on the table at the edge with his right hand. Shari watched how he paid attention to how close it lay from the side and how he removed a piece of lint that had fallen onto it. "We could probably put a football field down by the train station, but it would most likely flood and be a little out of the way for the townspeople."

"It's a beautiful little town you have here. It seems very quiet and peaceful."

Nodding, he reached for the ice water but then pulled his hand back. "Eureka hasn't always been quiet. It's had its fair share of excitement over the years."

"What do you mean?"

"It has a history, that's for sure."

"What kind of history?"

He smiled and waved her question away. "That can wait for later. You haven't answered my question."

Shari nodded in agreement and took a sip of her wine. "My great-grandmother went here when it was a school for girls."

"Which class?" He ran his right forefinger around the edge of his hat. In spite of his age, Shari thought his hands looked remarkably young and smooth.

"She graduated in 1924. She didn't talk a whole lot about it." She pulled the glass closer to her. "I think something happened back then that weighed heavily on her for the rest of her life."

"Oh." The man nodded. "That was an exciting year in Eureka." He chuckled and raised his eyebrows.

"My Granny Millie told me that was the year they won the Southern Basketball Championship." She smiled at the memory of how excited her great-grandmother would get telling her the story of that final game against Joplin Junior College. "It must have been something."

"To say the least."

Something in the way he said it bothered Shari, and she couldn't figure out if he wasn't too impressed with the school's achievements or if he had a story to tell. She frowned at the man. He clicked his tongue against the roof of his mouth and leaned against the table. A drop of sweat beaded up on the side of his glass and suddenly started rolling down the side, gathering up more perspiration as it went and picking up speed until it landed on the table and spread around the base where it rested on the surface. They both watched the tumbling drop in silence, each waiting for the other to start the conversation back up. He took a small napkin and put the glass on top of it.

"Wasn't that also the year of one of the big fires?" Shari took another sip of chardonnay, savoring the rich, buttery flavor.

The old man sucked his top lip behind his slightly-crooked bottom teeth colored with coffee stains. He smoothed a thick shock of silver hair off his forehead before resting his hand on the table beside his derby. Closing his eyes, he leaned his head back and touched his forehead with his fingertips. He snapped his eyes open, and Shari's hand twitched.

"Sure was. And the last full year of the school." He glanced up at her, and she could not move her eyes away. "Along with a few other things that nearly destroyed this quaint little town and that still threaten it today."

Shari pushed herself up in her chair. "Sounds intriguing."

"You could say that."

Wrinkling her eyebrows, Shari pushed herself back in her chair and let her palms slide across the tablecloth until she gripped the edge of the table. She took a deep breath through her nose, feeling her shoulders rise as her lungs expanded.

"Say what?"

The old man licked his lips and ran the back of his left hand along his jaw from under his ear to his chin several times, remaining silent. His eyes met hers, and his pronounced Adam's apple moved up and down as he swallowed. The right corner of his mouth curled up in a little half smile.

"A lot happened that spring," Kenneth said. "People lost fortunes, the fire ruined lives and exposed some rather devastating controversies."

Shari arched her brows and tilted her head. "Don't keep me in suspense." She leaned forward and rested her elbows on the table. "Please, tell me."

Kenneth pulled an antique-looking watch from his pocket. He opened the cover and glanced down at the time. "I guess I can. They don't close for a while."

"Thank you." Shari shifted in her seat and set her chin in her hands. "I always loved whenever my Granny Millie told us stories about the Crescent."

"All right." Nodding his head, the elderly man clicked his watch closed and put it back into his pocket. "This may take a little bit."

MONDAY, APRIL 7, 1924

*"...yet there the nightingale / Filled all the desert with inviolable voice /
And still she cries, and still the world pursues"*
—T.S. Eliot, *"The Waste Land."*

Mary took the damp cloth Elise offered and wiped it across her forehead. The girl's alabaster skin looked two shades whiter than normal. Her stomach grumbled in protest from the sip of water she had just swallowed, and her knees shook as she stood. Elise put an arm around her shoulders, holding her up while they hurried to the sink.

A wave of nausea enveloped Mary, and she stumbled. She reached out and grabbed the edge of the sink and pulled herself closer. Her stomach rumbled and she emptied its few contents into the basin.

"That's the third time this afternoon, honey." Elise wrinkled her brow and pushed Mary's hair back from her face. "Lie down. You can't play tonight."

"I have to." Mary's eyes widened, and she clutched at her chest. "Everybody—the school, even the town, my team—they're all depending on me. If we don't win, it has all been for nothing."

Elise took the cloth from her hand and wiped the edges of the girl's mouth. Then she set the cloth on the side of the sink. She frowned when Mary rolled her head over to look up at the elderly housemother.

"Playing Joplin in Kansas City makes us the underdogs, Miss Elise. They *need* me."

The older woman grinned and shook her head back and forth slowly. "I know, child. You lead the team in points, and for us to have any chance at all, you have to be on the court."

Mary nodded firmly. "Then it's settled."

"But you also have to be healthy, Mary." Elise put her hand on the top of Mary's shoulder. "You can't help them win if you're sick."

"I can do it." Mary sniffed and rubbed a fingertip at the corner of her mouth. "I'll be okay."

The housemother shook her head. "Why do you push yourself so, Mary Elizabeth Bencini?"

Mary shrugged. "I just have to."

"No, you don't." Elise tightened the grip on her shoulder. "Do you get this stubbornness from your father?"

"My father says I get it from my mother." Mary struggled to stand and could only manage a weak smile. "I like to think that part of her is in me."

Elise smiled softly. "Child, we are all pieces of our parents."

Nodding, Mary pushed herself away from the sink and ran her hand absently through her hair. She shook a little as she walked back to the locker room bench. "I'll be okay, Miss Elise."

"The game starts in three hours, Mary." The housemother stood there with her hands on her hips, jutting her chin out.

"They need me." She gazed at the elderly woman.

Elise pointed her finger and scowled at Mary. "If you throw up one more time, I'm going to get Dr. Lyttle."

Mary's eyes opened wide. She grabbed Elise's hand. "You mustn't, Miss Elise."

"Why not?" The housemother frowned at her.

She looked down and gripped the housemother's hands tighter. "Because he wouldn't allow me to play."

"Which is the way it should be."

Mary lowered her eyes and whispered, "This is the only thing I have. The other girls have their families and their vacations and their clothes. This is the only thing I have that is better than theirs."

"Oh, child." Elise hugged the girl tightly around her shoulders. "You have your whole life to live. Their money doesn't mean anything in the long run."

"I know." Mary smiled. "But it means something to me now. They only respect me when I'm helping them win."

She wished that it didn't mean anything, but everyone having nicer and more clothes than she did and talking about their trips to New York and Europe bothered her, making her feel like she was a foreigner wandering through a strange land.

Elise smiled and shook her head. "I don't know why you worry about those stuck up girls, Mary Elizabeth. But if you throw up one more time, I'm going to call the doctor. You've been throwing up every day for almost a week, now. You must've come down with something pretty serious."

Mary nodded and put her forehead against the housemother's shoulder. "Thank you, Miss Elise. Thank you."

A quiet tapping caused them to look around. The door opened and Joseph Goldman peeked around the edge. "How's my girl?"

Mary looked up. "I'm fine, Coach Goldman."

Joseph glanced at Elise and raised his right eyebrow. She saw the unspoken question between the two.

"She's okay for now, Mr. Goldman." Elise smoothed her dress and walked over to the door. "She's just got a little bug."

"Okay," Goldman said. "We were worried."

Joseph pulled his head back and let the door close behind him. Mary looked up at Elise and smiled weakly.

"Thank you," she whispered.

Elise nodded and headed toward the door. She stopped and turned just before she reached it. "Just you take it easy for now. But I'm telling you, I will call Dr. Lyttle. Try not to do too much."

She stopped and glanced up at the ceiling. "And you stay away from that J.W. Floyd, child. He is nothing but trouble."

Mary gasped, astonished that the housemother would have noticed her fascination with the young man. He had captured her interest from the moment she first saw him back when the fall semester began.

"But I think I love him, Miss Elise." She wrinkled the corners of her eyes and took several quick breaths through her nose.

"I know, child." The woman waggled a finger at her. "But you just take a lesson from your housemother and stay away. If you don't, little Miss Stuart could cause some trouble for you. She's been telling everyone that they're engaged."

—

"All right, Comets." Goldman motioned for the girls to gather around him at the sideline. "You have got to get Bencini open."

The Crescent Comets crowded around Coach Goldman and stole glances at the scoreboard—Wranglerettes 17-Comets 8 at the half. Phoebe took a quick drink of water and wiped sweat away from her eyes.

"I know they're taller than us." Coach Goldman lowered himself down in the huddle. "We've held them to only five offensive points."

"If Mary would quit giving the ball back to them." Phoebe glared at the smaller girl with her long blonde hair held away from her face with barrettes. She never could understand why Mary wouldn't just cut her hair short like all the other girls did. Those Catholics just didn't know anything about fashion.

"I know, Stuart." Goldman slashed his hand down in an arc. "We gave up twelve easy points."

Phoebe's smile faded quickly when Goldman defended the other girl. "But Bencini's not the only player out there on the court. You all need to step up. They are shutting us down offensively." The coach looked at the scoreboard. "Bencini only has four points. Find her for the open shot."

"She's slowing us down, Coach Goldman!" Phoebe hated it that she sounded like she was whining, but she still felt like the scrawny little urchin with her hand-me-down clothes didn't have what it took to come through in the end. "We can't get her open if she's still in the back court."

Goldman glanced over at Mary. "She's right, Bencini. You have got to pick it up, or I'm going to pull you."

Mary nodded but glared at Phoebe. She curled the right side of her lip in a sneer and closed her fingers into a fist at her. Phoebe pulled her head back, creasing her brow and opening her mouth to protest.

"Stuart!" he shouted.

Phoebe jumped and looked the coach in the eye. Goldman remained silent for a moment, tapping the side of his leg and waiting for the other girls to pay attention.

"Yes, Coach Goldman?"

"You need to drive a lot harder to the basket." The man pushed his hands forward with the fingers together like a wedge.

When she opened her mouth to protest, he held his right hand up with one finger pointing at her. She huffed and slumped her shoulders.

He lowered his head and looked at her from under his brows. "They're not buying your attack. Make them real and dish off at the last moment if they close on you."

"What if they don't close?"

Goldman shrugged. "Be a hero. Take the shot."

He stood up and smoothed his jacket. "Now, let's get this game won. Get back out there and do some damage."

The Comets all shouted in agreement and jumped out on the court, ready to play. Phoebe glanced across the court and shook her head when she saw Mary grab her side and grimace. The roar of the crowd thundered through the arena, echoing off the rafters and rattling the windows. It had taken a lot of time and a lot of hard work to get to the Southern Basketball Championship, and Phoebe decided that she wasn't going to let a chauffeur's daughter ruin things for all of them.

The referee gave Mildred the ball, and she inbounded it to Phoebe. She took the ball and dribbled down the right side of the court. Crossing over to the top of the key, she noticed that the defense played her soft and settled back to defend against Mary. Swallowing, she took a quick gasp of breath and moved toward the basket.

Only one defender stepped into the lane to try to cut her off, but she switched to the other hand and drove around the Wranglerette. She put the ball up and held her breath as it bounced off the backboard and rolled completely around the rim before dropping through.

Even though they were outnumbered four-to-one, the Comets' fans cheered so loudly that Phoebe even heard someone shout her own name. She beamed with pride and jumped for the ball, knocking it back out of bounds. The next ball went over her head toward half court, but Mary stepped in front of the pass and quickly threw the ball back to Phoebe. She caught the ball and froze momentarily, surprised, then shot it.

The ball came off the backboard too hard and bounced down off the front of the rim, but Mildred caught it coming down the lane and hit the layup. Once facing a hopeless situation, the Comets had suddenly closed to within five points with less than a minute off the clock.

—

Mary looked up at the time as she caught the inbound pass from Mildred. With a little over two minutes left in the game, the Comets trailed 28-24, but she'd made four shots in a row to lead them on an eight-to-nothing run. Phoebe had been doing just what the coach had asked. The Wranglerettes realized they couldn't give her the lane without contesting her, which freed Mary to take the open shots.

She came down the court and passed the ball behind her to Phoebe. The other girl drove and dropped the ball off to Mildred, who snapped the ball back to Mary at the top of the key. The ball sailed just as quickly from Mary's hands, sinking through the rim to pull the Comets within two points.

Mildred stood taller, but was slower, than any other Comet, but she used a surprising burst of speed to cut in front of the inbound pass and immediately put the ball back up. It hit the backboard, then dropped straight through the basket. The dominant Joplin crowd was stunned into silence, while the Comets' fans cheered wildly and stomped their feet, rattling the grayed-out widows around the gymnasium.

With the score tied 28-28, the Wranglerettes didn't take any chances and moved the ball slowly down the court. Phoebe met the player with the ball at the top of the key and swatted at it but hit only air. The ball sailed over her head to a wide-open girl under the basket. Both teams watched the ball roll around the rim as they fought for position. Mildred jumped higher than the other players and grabbed the ball as it skipped off the rim.

She came down and then passed it to Phoebe toward the sideline between two defenders. Phoebe whipped it up the court to Mary racing down the floor. She caught the ball, dribbled twice and laid the ball off the backboard to give the Comets the lead for the first time in the game. Joplin inbounded the ball and put it up at half court, but the desperation shot never came close. Mary looked over at the scorecards as the clock ticked down to zero with the Comets up 30-28.

Standing alone at half court, she watched as the Comets' fans poured onto the court, cheering and waving wildly. Her teammates ran over to her, and she felt a little overwhelmed as they closed her view of the arena around her. She tried to remain calm, but the excitement infected her with a comforting sense of joy and exhilaration.

She hugged Mildred back when the girl grabbed her, shouting just as loud and jumping just as high as her teammate. They laughed so hard that Mary had to blink repeatedly to see through all the tears. Several strange people hugged her, and she hugged them back just as hard. The upset stomach and nausea had long since passed, replaced by the warm excitement caused by winning the championship game.

Mary looked up and sucked in a quick little gasp when she saw J.W.'s slim form stop in front of her. His clear blue eyes shone beneath his black hair.

"Great job, Mary." She just knew her heart had skipped a beat when she heard her name with his voice.

She looked up at him and felt a warm rush creep up her neck and over her face. He smiled, showing perfect white teeth. She couldn't find her voice and only nodded.

"I'm serious, Mary." He smiled broadly, putting his hand on her shoulder to steady himself from all the jostling around them. "They couldn't have done it without you."

"Thank you, J.W." Her voice sounded timid and squeaky to her.

"You're a hero, Mary." His compliment made her blush and turn away.

John William Floyd III had grabbed Mary's attention from the first moment she had seen him last autumn, coming to the school with Phoebe and her family. His father owned the Western Lumber Company—the largest supplier of lumber in the nation, and they had also bought up much of the best real estate in Eureka Springs. They lived in a large brownstone mansion in Garfield west of Eureka. J.W. was also courting Phoebe Stuart, whose family owned several large oil wells in the Texas panhandle and southwestern Oklahoma and donated large sums of money to several political organizations. Mary knew she couldn't compete with the girl's family money or her thick red hair, ivory skin, and blue eyes.

But Mary felt certain that she loved J.W., and would do almost anything to have him return that feeling. She shivered when he put his strong arms around her shoulders in a fierce bear hug. When Mary looked over J.W.'s shoulder, she saw Phoebe glaring at her from the sidelines. Mary closed her eyes, shutting out the girl's jealous stare, and rested her cheek on his shoulder.

He released her from the hug and walked over to talk to the school president Richard Thompson. A thin, elderly man in a rumpled gray suit with no tie caught her attention. All through her childhood, Mary could not remember her father looking so old. Before she came to Eureka Springs for school, she couldn't remember her father's appearance changing at all from one year to the next. Wrinkles at the corners of his eyes now etched deep valleys in his skin, and the skin on his neck seemed loose and flabby like a turkey's wattle.

She left the rest of her team and sprinted over to the stands, jumping up to hug the man around his neck as he stepped onto the floor. "What are you doing here, Daddy?"

Carmine Bencini smiled softly, looking at her. Gray streaked his black hair at the temples, and the edges of his brown eyes were rimmed with red. Tears welled up and almost spilled down his cheek. He grabbed her tightly to his chest and rocked her back and forth.

"Senator and Mrs. Mitchell are staying in town this week." He pulled a white handkerchief out of his inside jacket pocket and wiped at his eyes. "They let me come over to watch the game."

Mary smiled widely and took his hand in her own. "Did you see me play?"

Her father smiled and ruffled her sweat-streaked hair. "Of course I did, my flower. And I saw every single one of your twenty points."

"Come meet everyone, Daddy," she pleaded, tugging at his arm.

Carmine pulled his arm free and grasped his daughter's shoulders. She looked up at his suddenly serious face and frowned.

"What is it, Daddy?" Her stomach started to flutter with nervousness, and she narrowed her eyes.

He smiled softly, giving her shoulders a quick squeeze, and then reached into his side jacket pocket. He pulled out a gold locket shaped like a quarter moon—the same shape adorning the cobblestone walkway in front of the Crescent—that hung from a delicate chain.

Gently, he undid the clasp and reached to put it around her neck. Mary gasped quietly and held her hand over her mouth.

"Is this mama's locket?" Her skin flushed and the warmth spread down her neck and across her chest. Her lungs hurt, and she had to pull hard at each breath to keep from fainting. She spun around so he could see to get the chain together.

"Yes. I think you're old enough to have it now." Carmine turned her around and looked first at the locket against her sweaty uniform and then into her eyes, smiling.

She clapped her hands together quickly several times like a little girl with a new toy, and then kissed her father on the cheek. The gym lights reflected off the locket and flashed across Carmine's face and eyes. He turned away for a moment, and when he brought his hand to his face, she knew he was trying to wipe away the tears before she could see them.

"Thank you, Daddy." She held the locket between her thumb and forefinger, watching as the lights reflected off the gold surface. "This is the best present I have ever had."

Her father reached out and touched her cheek with his fingertips. "I'm glad you like it, Mary Elizabeth."

She studied the locket longer. Carmine Bencini had given it to her mother—Virginia Hutchingson of Salisbury, England—as a present on their wedding night. They were both immigrants and had met on Ellis Island. Their courtship only lasted two weeks after becoming citizens and, since neither of them had family in the United States, they decided to move to St. Louis. In less than a year of marriage, Virginia became pregnant with Mary.

It had been a hard pregnancy with Virginia nearly miscarrying several times. When it came time to deliver, Virginia had told Carmine the name she wanted and told him that she would love him forever. She died two minutes after the midwife had placed their infant daughter in her arms. Even though their marriage had lasted less than two years, he never had any interest in marrying another woman. Mary never knew her mother and would have liked for her father to have someone in his life to care for him, but she loved him all the more for loving Virginia so fiercely.

Mary turned the locket over and read the inscription there, even though she had seen it many times before. "For my heart—my Virginia."

Carmine smiled, his eyes still moist. "She would have wanted you to have it. She would want you to have its protection."

She turned the locket back over and clutched it against her chest. "Thank you, Daddy."

Behind her, Goldman called to the Comets, trying to gather them around so that they could accept the trophy. Mary looked around, then back at her father.

He nodded, grinning. "Go on."

As she returned to the huddle, Carmine called after her. "I'll be down Thursday, Mary. You be careful."

Mary waved and blew him a kiss. She sat down on the bench beside the rest of her teammates. They laughed and smiled, jostling each other playfully. Goldman came over with the silver cup and kneeled down in front of them.

He blinked repeatedly before he could manage to get any sounds to come out of his throat. "This is the result of coming together as a team. You are all good athletes by yourselves, but you are so much better as a team."

Several of the girls nodded, and Mildred reached over to pat Mary on the back. She smiled at Mary and nodded once.

"Now, let's get home." Goldman clapped his hands together and stood up. "You still have classes tomorrow."

The girls moaned half-heartedly and began to wander back to the locker room. Even with the threat of little sleep in class the next day, they still filled the gym with triumphant shouts and laughter. Mary had nearly reached her locker when she felt someone poke her sharply in the back. She turned and saw Phoebe smiling closed-lip at her.

"Enjoy it," she sneered. "Even a driver's daughter can be a hero sometimes."

Mary looked over Phoebe's shoulder at Richard Thompson, who glared sternly at the other girl's back. He cleared his throat and Phoebe started, whirling to face the school president.

"Now, Phoebe." He talked to her like he would a small child, but there was no sternness in his expression. "You know that this school does not tolerate class-segregation."

Phoebe nodded, looking down at the floor. "Yes, sir."

"You need to correct that behavior." He headed toward the exit with the rest of the fans.

Phoebe sniffed, looking at Mary before following Goldman and the rest of the Comets into the locker room. Mary took one last look down the hall at the quickly emptying arena and sighed. With the season over, there was no reason for the other girls to like her.

———

Mildred pulled the covers back on her bed in the cabin that she shared with Phoebe and Mary. After a quick dinner, the Comets and many of their fans caught the 11:55 out of Kansas City to Seligman, Missouri. She usually bunked with Phoebe and Irene Jones, but Irene had permission to stay with her family the rest of the week. Mary had been appointed to their cabin at the last minute.

She knew Phoebe despised Mary, but she did not have a problem with the girl herself. If Phoebe behaved as usual, Mildred knew the overnight train ride back home would be filled with misery and petty jealousy. Mildred yawned as she climbed into the bottom bunk.

Mary entered the room in a white flannel nightgown, carrying her toothbrush and toothpowder in her hands. She walked over to the bunk opposite Mildred's and put the items in her gym bag. Above Mildred, Phoebe sat up and swung her legs over the edge.

"I saw you hug J.W." Phoebe fixed Mary with an accusing stare.

"He hugged me." Mary turned away from Phoebe and looked like she was about to break into tears, frowning and her bottom lip quivering.

Shaking her head, Mildred defended their class and teammate. "He hugged the whole team, Phoebe. Even me. Are you going to get mad at me, too?"

"That's not the point!" Phoebe glared at Mildred. "She hugged him back."

"So?" Mildred shrugged and grinned. "He's handsome. I hugged him back as well. He has strong arms."

Phoebe hopped off the bunk and jabbed a finger at her face. "Are you on her side, now?"

"Oh, shut up, Phoebe." Mildred pulled the covers over her shoulders. "Forget about it. Go to sleep."

She rolled over to face the cabin wall and tucked her hands under the pillow. She felt Phoebe step on her bunk to climb back up to her own bed.

After a brief silence, Phoebe said, her voice full of venom, "Just remember, Mary. You may like him because he's beautiful, but he's going to marry me."

Mildred twisted over and looked across the compartment at Mary. The moon just three days past full cast enough light through the window that she could easily see the poor girl's tears glistening like diamonds as they tumbled down her cheeks. She sat at the edge of her bed staring out the window. Her shoulders rose and fell with each breath, but every few inhales her body shuddered.

Being raised with no mother could not be an easy thing, Mildred imagined. Her own mother had always been there every step of her life. She wrote her every week while away at school. When she went home for the summer, they would sit in the garden and drink lemonade together while her younger siblings played marbles or tossed a baseball back and forth. Her mother always listened to her and gave her advice when she had questions. Mildred hated how Phoebe constantly mocked Mary for never going on vacations and being the child of a serving man rather than having servants. Her own mother always told her the importance of never looking down on someone that had less, that you must be thankful for your blessings and that you should help those less fortunate.

Mildred could not imagine being without her mother. The Thorton household would not be the same without her mother there. In fact, Mildred didn't think she would be the same person if it wasn't for the friendship she shared with her mother. Mary didn't have anyone like that, and Phoebe relentlessly invoked the fact the girl had no mother and no money, airing it out like dirty laundry.

Mary closed her eyes and sniffed. She still gripped her toothbrush and powder in her hand, pulling her knees under her chin and pushing back into the shadows against the wall. Mildred could only see the girl's feet. Phoebe shifted around in the bunk above her, grunting and obviously not finding the ride very comfortable.

Served her right. Mildred rolled to her back and stared at the steel bands beneath the mattress.

"Hurry." She jumped at Phoebe's urgent, hissed whisper. "We have to see if this works."

Mildred pushed herself up onto one elbow. "What are you blathering about now, Phoebe? We need to get some sleep. We're not going to get enough before lessons as it is."

Phoebe grunted as she hopped down from her bunk and started rustling through her bag. "Where is it?"

"Where is what?" Mildred leaned over, watching as Phoebe pulled out several changes of clothes and set them on the bed. "Another set of clothes since you needed your whole wardrobe for a three-day trip?"

"The talking board, of course." Phoebe flashed a tight-lipped smile. "Did you forget we were going to try it tonight?"

Mildred let out a long sigh. "Honestly, Phoebe. I'm really tired and just want to go to sleep."

Her friend pouted. "You said we could do this." She pulled a plank of wood engraved with letters and numbers across it. "Yes!" She set the board on Mildred's bed and rummaged through her bag until she pulled a wooden planchette out and set it beside the plank.

"Where did you hear about this, Phoebe?" Mildred sat up and scooted away from the board.

Phoebe's obsession over the spiritual and modern trends always seemed to mix and mash about until something completely unexpected came out. She never knew what Phoebe would come up with next. She talked of a secular revolution with liberated thinking and in the very next breath spoke about the impact of other-worldly beings on the physical realm.

"My brother brought it down from Cleveland during the winter break."

Her excitement over the little piece of wood energized Mildred enough to relieve her drowsiness. It infected her more with a sense of annoyance rather than any eager anticipation. With the plank in one hand and the planchette in the other, Phoebe sat down cross-legged beneath the compartment window. The moon cast its pale, silvery light over her shoulder, and she set the board in front of her away from her shadow.

"Are you going to come down here?" Phoebe pulled the hem of her nightgown over her knees and rubbed her hands together like a small child about to open a present.

Mildred wrinkled her nose. "Nah. I'll just watch from here."

She looked over at the other bed. Mary hadn't moved, her face still hidden in the darkness. Mildred hoped Mary could see her, and she smiled what she hoped was an understanding smile.

"Do you want to participate in this adventure, Mary?" Phoebe glanced up from the floor. When Mary didn't answer, Phoebe shrugged. "You don't know what you're missing. My brother says the things the talking board can do are quite amazing."

Mary remained silent. Her feet moved even further from the edge of the bed. The only sound was the train clanking over the rails.

Phoebe's shoulders slumped a little. "I'm sorry, Mary."

Mildred swallowed and leaned back. Phoebe Stuart never apologized. Not unless she wanted something.

"I know I get a little cranky at times." Phoebe pursed her lips. "My brother even says I'm too spoiled. Will you forgive my rudeness?"

From the shadows, Mary cleared her throat. "That's okay. I'll just watch."

"Fine." Phoebe's response was short and clipped. Mildred knew the apology wasn't heartfelt. Phoebe got what Phoebe wanted. Simple as that.

"Now observe everything carefully." Phoebe placed the planchette on the board, settling her first two fingers of each hand at the wide end of the piece.

Mildred leaned over. "What do you do?"

"Ask it a question and then wait for the answer."

"Does it actually talk to you?" Mary's voice sounded strained.

Phoebe shook her head. "No, silly. It moves your hands and spells out the answers to your questions."

"What?" Mildred couldn't believe that some little plank of wood would know the answers of some unprepared, obscure question. "That sounds a little hokey, if you ask me."

"Well, I'm not." The other girl shrugged. "My brother said the piece will move your hands and spell out the answers."

"What moves your hands?"

"I don't know." Phoebe sounded irritated now, but Mildred couldn't figure out how the board worked.

"Is it imbued with some spirit? Possessed by something from the other side?" She made her voice tremble like she thought it should when someone read Edgar Allen Poe's *The Raven*.

"I said I don't know, Mildred." Phoebe's voice rose at the end, becoming harsh. "Just watch. Maybe it's magic."

None of them spoke for a few moments. The rumbling of the train and clacking of the wheels over the rails filled Mildred's ears. She could feel the vibrations in her hands when she gripped the side of her bunk, and they ran up her arms. If she relaxed her jaw muscles, the trembling would set her teeth to chattering like they would on winter mornings when the fire had gone out during the night.

"It sounds devilish." Mary moved her feet further into the shadows as if she were trying to get even further away from them. "Be careful."

Phoebe laughed. "You girls are silly."

"I don't know, Phoebe," Mary said. "This doesn't seem too smart doing something that you don't know much about. What if there is some evil attached to it?"

"Just watch." Phoebe coughed once and hunched her shoulders over the board. Her back rose as she took a deep breath, and then sank when she exhaled loud enough Mildred could hear the air escape through her pursed lips.

"What does the future hold for us?"

Mildred opened her mouth and gasped. "Why would you want to know that, Phoebe?"

"Shh," Phoebe snapped through gritted teeth, her head jerking to the side.

The little piece of wood beneath her fingers started to move around the board. Mildred and Mary both gasped, while Phoebe just grinned. It started out in wide circles that shrunk with each revolution, speeding up as it tightened until it stopped with the point indicating the F. The circles widened and began the process all over, resting on the I. The next time the planchette stopped, it pointed at the R.

"Look, Phoebe." Mildred laughed even though she still felt more nervous than excited about the whole thing. "It can't even spell furs. Didn't you want a mink for Christmas last year?"

Phoebe shook her head and grunted as the piece started moving again. When the tightening circle stopped, the point rested on the E.

Phoebe sounded confused. "What does fire have to do with our future?"

Mildred shrugged and then realized that neither of the other girls could probably see her. "I don't know. We just had a pretty cold winter."

Before Phoebe could answer or Mary add any of her own suggestions, the piece started its rotating sweep over the board. The point ended above the D.

"E," Mary said after the next letter.

When it stopped for the third time, Mildred said, "A."

Phoebe called out the fourth letter. "T."

Mary and Mildred both scrambled to the edges of their bunks, looking down at the board as Phoebe hunched over it. Her fingers, set so delicately on the wooden piece, moved about in ever shrinking circles until the point stopped directly above the H.

"Death," Phoebe whispered.

She looked at the talking board, rocking back and forth slowly. Mildred wondered if her friend wanted the piece to start moving again to spell something else or to add an explanation just like she did. But the calm voice came from Mary, something solid in the dim compartment lit only by the moon flashing in and out from between the trees.

"Death comes to us all." She picked her feet up off the floor and lay down on her bed. "That's not much of a fortune-telling board you have there, Phoebe."

Phoebe just stared at the board beneath her. The planchette remained motionless. Mildred couldn't imagine what Phoebe must be thinking. Her friend had never known a hardship in her life. In spite of her stubborn independence and unpleasant attitude toward anyone that didn't measure up to her standards, Phoebe would probably end up being the most successful out of all of them. J.W. had the right idea in tying himself to the Stuarts by marriage—even if Phoebe did have some ideas about marriage and women's rights that seemed out of sorts to the Victorian sensibilities of Mildred's own family.

"Mary's right," she said. "That's nothing that doesn't happen to every single person that has ever walked this earth."

"I guess." Phoebe pulled her legs under her and sat on her knees. "I just thought it would be something different. My brother never told me he experienced anything like this."

Mildred suddenly smelled something pungent and bitter almost like mothballs, and her nose wrinkled. "Did you spill something in your bag, Phoebe?"

"No. I don't think so." Pheobe reached over and grabbed her purse. "I smell it, too."

"What is it?"

Something hit the narrow top window of their compartment from the outside, sending a shower of glass all over the floor. The wind started to scream through the opening. Mildred winced and covered her ears. She knew she was screaming herself but couldn't hear her own voice over the deafening screech of the sound whistling through the shattered window.

Mary had rolled off the bunk and sat with her back against the compartment door. She had her knees tucked up under her chin. Her hands covered her ears, and her mouth gaped wide as if she too was screaming. But Mildred couldn't hear Mary's voice either. The other girl had pulled her neck muscles taut as if they strained to keep her head attached, and veins bulged against the skin. Her fingers had started to dig into the side of her head, and her knuckles whitened. She rolled away from the door, curled into a ball.

Mildred struggled to stand and staggered over to the compartment door. She flipped the lock open and slid the door back. She looked out in the passageway and saw a conductor running toward them, the light from his swinging short-globe lantern glowing and shimmering. Still tying the belt of her bathrobe, Miss Elise nearly crashed into the trainman when she burst from her own compartment.

The conductor stepped roughly past Mildred and held his lantern up to shine into the room. She looked over the man's shoulder and saw Phoebe standing in front of the window. Her arms spread from one top bunk to the other. She grinned as if the shrieking didn't disturb her. Her hair spread out like a halo of flame around her head. In the window, Mildred caught the reflection of another shape poised to leap from the bunk onto Phoebe.

"Look out!" She lunged into the room.

When she tackled Phoebe to the floor, the large compartment windows shattered and blew out of the room, crashing into the forest beside the tracks. Just as suddenly as it had started, the whistling stopped. The only sounds were the rushing of the wind past the ruined window and Mary's fading screams. Mildred rolled off Phoebe and jerked her head around, following the conductor's light and casting her gaze into every corner of the compartment. She did not see anything besides the three of them and the conductor.

Miss Elise stood in the entry, a frown etched across her brow. She knelt down and put her arms around Mary. The girl shivered, and Mildred felt like doing the same.

"What happened?" Miss Elise shouted over the wind. "What have you two done to Mary?"

Mildred shook her head, eyes widened in disbelief. "Nothing, Miss Elise."

Their housemother squinted her eyes. "Do you expect me to believe that?"

"I—" Mildred started to answer, but she could only swallow a couple of breaths.

Phoebe pushed herself off the floor. "She got scared, Miss Elise." Her shoulders shrugged, and she reached up and smoothed her red locks against her head.

Mildred couldn't believe how Phoebe could be so calm. They had just spoken to some spirit or some other power through the talking board, and Phoebe acted as if nothing unusual had happened.

"We were talking about the game." Phoebe looked at Mary where the girl trembled against Miss Elise, clutching at the housemother's robe in one hand and holding the other against her own chest. "I was just telling Mary how the town will probably have a celebration for us. And then the window just broke and made this awful noise."

The housemother looked down at Mary, stroking her hair. "Is this true, child?"

Mary blinked several times before looking over her shoulder at Phoebe. Then she glanced at Mildred, but she could only shrug. "I guess so, Miss Elise. The noise just frightened me something terrible."

Miss Elise looked back and forth between Mildred and Phoebe before reaching down to Mary. "Okay, child. Let's get you girls to some beds and let this nice gentleman clean up in here."

"Yes, Miss Elise," Mary mumbled so quietly that Mildred barely heard her.

"Found it." Behind them, the conductor had knelt down and looked under the bunk where Mary had been set to sleep.

"Found what, young man?" Miss Elise glowered.

He reached under the bunk and pulled out the carcass of a small screech owl. "What must have broken the window. Perhaps its cries are what the girls heard."

Flicking her gaze from Mildred and back to Phoebe, Miss Elise nodded a couple of times. She helped Mary to her feet. "Has this kind of thing ever happened before, sir?"

The conductor pushed his bottom lip out and shrugged. "Sure. Lots of birds hit the windows at night. I think they see the reflection of the moon in the window and try to fly through them. Never had one break the window before."

A reflection. That is what Mildred had seen, only whatever it had been was no longer in the room. She didn't think it could have jumped out of the speeding train. Where could it have hidden? She knelt down and glanced under the bunks, studying the shadows to see if anything hid in their depths. Next, she climbed up and looked on both top bunks.

"What are you looking for, child?" Miss Elise glared at Mildred, her voice taut and impatient like on those mornings when the girls were late getting around.

She turned and winced at the older woman's scowl. "My bag." She stammered out the answer. Miss Elise tapped her foot against the floor, and Mildred saw her bag next to the woman's feet.

"Ah," she said. She walked over and grabbed it by the handle. With her head lowered, she walked to the compartment door behind Phoebe. Miss Elise helped a quivering Mary, and Mildred took another quick glance behind the conductor but didn't see anything.

Miss Elise had a compartment of her own but still had four beds. She gave the three empty ones to the girls. Phoebe and Mildred took the top bunks, while Mary crawled into the one of the lower berths. Their housemother fussed over all three of them but spent a little extra time with Mary, who still hadn't said a word since they'd left their own room. She huddled in her bed with the blankets tucked up under her chin. Her eyes kept glancing to the door and the window, and her shoulders twitched at every sound louder than a whisper.

Phoebe stirred above her, and Mary grimaced, rolling to her side with her back against the bulkhead and her knees pulled up to her chest. The car swayed side-to-side a little on the track as the train lumbered up onto the Ozark Plateau. Sitting on the edge of the bed, Miss Elise stroked Mary's hair and hummed a wordless tune that soon had Mildred fighting to keep her own eyes open.

Just before she drifted off to sleep, Mildred thought she heard Phoebe mumble something in the bunk across from her. She put her head at the edge of the bed but didn't hear anything else. The last thing she remembered thinking about was winning the trophy in the basketball game. They had worked hard the entire season and had believed in the vision Coach Goldman shared with them. They awoke pulling into the Seligman station, and the sky had lightened to the dim gray twilight between the dark and the day. The remnants of a couple of troubling dreams drifted out of reach from Mildred, and she couldn't pull them back again.

A couple of stars still burned deep in the western sky, and the first fingers of the sunrise crept above the hills to the east by the time the cars pulled into the lot in front of the college. Mildred shuffled out of the car, dragging her bag with her and trying to keep her eyes open and make it safely up to her room. They had a couple hours before breakfast and their first classes. She hoped two hours of uninterrupted sleep would give her enough energy to get her through the day. Though Phoebe had the room next to hers, the two friends didn't say a word to each other. Mildred didn't bother to unpack before throwing herself onto her bed and falling asleep as soon as she closed her eyes.

―

Lionel Peterson walked down the center aisle of the church between the rows of wooden pews with kneeling benches. The faint scent of incense still floated on the air, probably left from the afternoon Wednesday Mass given by Monsignor Rafael Peretti. The hard leather heels of his box-toe oxfords knocked against the floor as he crossed the nave. He knelt in front of the sanctuary, and after quickly crossing himself, he stepped over the low railing and ducked into the radiating chapel off the southeast wall.

The afternoon sun did not light up the stained glass here, so the colors and images were muted and quiet, not at all like they would be in the early morning when it would strike the glass and bring out every sharp detail. He walked straight over to the unadorned, gray stone altar nearest the outside wall. A deep staircase cut through the stone foundation led down into the earth from the narrow space between the altar and the side of the building.

He took a lantern off the shelf at the bottom of the stairs. The match flared brightly, and the smell of phosphorus burned his nose. He lifted the chimney and set the flame against the wick. It caught, and he lowered it enough to keep the light from glaring too harshly in the dim passage.

At the end of the short hallway, he came to a broad door set in a rounded frame and hanging from ancient-looking, black iron hinges. He tugged open the door, wincing when it let out a sharp little squeak like someone had just stepped on a mouse. Beyond the door, he found a wide chamber set with lines of bookshelves reaching up toward the ceiling.

A gray light drifted down among the rows of shelves from the narrow, stained glass windows near the top of the walls where the vaulted ceiling started to arch up into a deeper dimness. Lionel walked quickly along the aisles, his heels striking against the stone floor, but the air felt thick and weighted so that each step sounded dull and muffled. Quick glances at the shelves revealed obscure titles, many of them in Latin or some tongue other than the English spoken by himself and the curator. Some of the texts still bore the damage they took when the cyclone of 1896 swept through the St. Louis area and flooded part of the cathedral and the chambers beneath it.

Lionel called out after he turned onto the next aisle. "Greetings, old friend."

He could barely discern the shape of a man from the shadows hunched over a desk at the far end. After a few seconds of silence, the shape straightened and turned around. "I recognize a voice from my past. How are you, Lionel?"

"Well, Mr. Erik Penman," he answered, chuckling. "I always thought that a perfect surname for the curator of ancient texts and codices at Saints Peter and Paul."

"Names have meaning," the other man replied. "Who are you this time?"

He smiled as he approached, making sure to lower the light on his lamp even more than he had already. Erik kept the libraries dim because he felt too much light could ruin the delicate parchments. "Detective Lionel Peterson of the Eureka Springs Police Department. Recently transferred from Chicago."

The stooped curator shrugged. "Interesting." He turned his attention back to the book spread open on the desk.

"I thought you might like it." He set the lantern down on the table in the middle of the vestibule. "There is a mystery afoot."

Erik grunted. "You always have liked the unknown."

Lionel shrugged. "It's just my nature." He started looking up and down the shelves, stopping and squinting to read the titles in the gloomy light.

"I doubt that," Erik said. He frowned at Lionel, grabbing his coat sleeve and turning him around. "Let me get a closer look at you."

After studying him for a minute, Erik shook his head. "You look as if you haven't aged one bit. Did you find a good woman to take care of you?"

Lionel laughed. "No woman would have me. Too much time out of the house."

"That is certainly true." The other man scratched at his forehead. "Father Peretti keeps telling me that since I don't take the time to look for a wife, I should have just joined the priesthood."

"Why did you never take your vows?"

Erik shrugged and lifted his wire-framed glasses to put them on. "I could have, I guess."

He picked the book off his desk in front of him and held it up into a spot just a little brighter than the rest of the room, squinting as he searched the words. "It was the celibacy part that always held me back."

Barking a quick laugh, Lionel clasped the other man on the shoulder. "You're a lover of books, Erik. What woman would not feel as if she were competing with Aeneas and Zacharias for your affections?"

The gray-haired man set the book back on the desk with a huff, and dust puffed up in eddies that swirled in the air, curling back onto the surface. Erik smiled and clapped his hands together. "I don't know. I thought that maybe one day I might be of interest to someone."

Lionel gave the man's shoulder a quick squeeze. "There is still time. You have years in you yet."

The curator shrugged. "Sure. I'm a real catch, I tell you." He curled his lip and with his left forefinger scratched at his earlobe.

Lionel dropped his hand and turned back to the rows of books and scrolls. He found what he was looking for and took down a tome titled *Theophrastus* from a nearby shelf and flipped it open to the middle of the book. He set the book on the table beside the lantern so he could read it. From the corner of his eye, he saw Erik's lips pull tight and his brow wrinkle.

Erik frowned at him, his eyes narrowing and searching Lionel's face as if he hoped to find some answers hidden in the details. "I was younger than you the last time we worked together. You came to St. Louis telling us that the cyclone twenty-eight years ago was not of this world."

"And it wasn't." Lionel hated this part. Some people could never get used to being around the *upper ones*. They often read from rote very well about the presence of beings not belonging on the Earth but could never seem to grasp the actual, physical concept of it.

"How'd you not age?"

Blunt. Lionel liked that. This conversation might not be as hard as he had originally feared. He shrugged. "I guess we do. Just not in the same way as you."

The side of Erik's cheek puffed out as he pushed his tongue between his teeth and squinted his eyes. After a moment, he clicked his tongue and nodded. "Fine. I knew you probably weren't..." He stood up from his chair and spread his arms wide in front of him. "Human."

Shaking his head slowly, Lionel curled his lips in a soft smile. "You're right. And I need your help."

Erik raised his eyebrows. "Really?"

Lionel nodded. "You know these books and their contents better than anyone ever has. I need to find out if what I am going to face in Eureka Springs could be the same thing we fought in 1896."

In the dim light, Erik ran his fingers up either side of his face. He grimaced and scratched his fingers back and forth over his scalp. "Is that why you are here? Are you chasing something again?"

He nodded. "For these past couple months I have felt something is about to happen."

"Okay. Then you better get to the point instead of dancing all around it. What do you need to know?"

Smiling, Lionel turned the flame up on the lamp in spite of the curator's frown. He never felt as comfortable reading in the dim light as the curator. "You never know." He put his finger on the pages of the book. "Seriously though, Aeneas wrote that the soul is eternal. But what of the Fallen?"

Erik moved to the shelves behind him. "But why ask about the Fallen?"

Lionel shook his head, grimacing. "I just feel we have faced this before. A long time ago."

"I see." The curator nodded slowly, and then continued searching the shelves. He stretched to his greatest height and struggled a brief second or two before pulling a thin volume off the top shelf.

"Lucius Heroditimus mentions that Aeneas and other Neoplatonic philosophers were correct about both the world and souls being eternal," Erik said between grunts. "He never comes right out and says anything about the Fallen but does reference a passage from *De Sphaeris In Bello* that the war between the spheres runs through cycles and that each one has been fought and will be fought again."

He set the narrow manuscript down on the table and thumbed through the pages, quickly at first, slowing until he found the page he wanted. With his finger on the text, he pointed at the words and read. "*Tamen certamine victus hostis erit usque ad adventum Domini identidem.*"

"My Latin is a bit rusty."

"My enemy has been defeated yet we shall contest again and again until our Lord returns."

Lionel looked over at him. "What else?"

Erik shrugged. "Nothing." He closed the book. "Like I said, that passage is actually taken from *De Sphaeris In Bello…The War of the Spheres*. Heroditimus didn't even write it. Several ancient writers mention it, but not one reveals the author or purpose of the text."

Nodding, Lionel watched as the curator put the book back. "So I could be facing something I have seen before."

"Sure. You never know."

"Thank you, brother." He closed the Theophrastus book before returning it to its spot on the shelf. "It is always enlightening to visit with you."

"Go in peace, my friend."

Lionel snorted and shook his head. "I have a feeling this one is going to be one of the worst."

He picked the lamp up off the desk and walked back toward the library entrance. His steps sounded even more muffled and short than when he had entered the vaults. The reason for his visit had been to maybe find something that would tell him what he would be facing after he arrived in Eureka Springs. But he still had one more thing to pick up from the chambers beneath the cathedral overhead.

The heavy oak door swung into place behind him, and he set off down the hall. After making several turns down corridors that grew more and more narrow and the ceilings dropped so low that he felt his head would brush the timbers any moment, he came to an iron door at the end of one passage.

Breathing in deeply and letting the air escape his lungs slowly, he closed his eyes. When he opened them, his shoulders relaxed. The tension across his back had grown slowly enough that he had not recognized it until just now, standing in front of the door. He could not take these next steps with any reservations. He needed to be committed and ready.

Reaching out slowly, he grasped the metal ring in the center of the door and pulled. The muscles in his shoulders and the backs of his legs strained, and he could feel the weight in the door shift as it swung outward. Air rushed into the room, pulled from the hall behind him and pushing his hair onto his ear.

No light from the corridor breached the threshold, and the room behind the door remained cloaked in darkness. He reached into the space with his right arm up to his shoulder, knowing what he would find, and gripped his hand firmly around the hilt. The sword, silver from the tip of the blade to the end of the pommel, followed his arm out of the room. It seemed to magnify the feeble light from the lamp in Lionel's other hand and illuminated the stones of the corridor.

It didn't matter how long between the various conflicts, the weight and heft of the sword always felt familiar, comfortable. Made over fifteen hundred years ago in Syria, the blade had never dulled or tarnished. Many lives had been saved when he had used it in the past. Many more had been taken to protect the others. He did not feel this time would be any different.

He set the lamp on the ground and pulled out a cloth sack that he used to cover the sword. After wrapping a cord around it and securing it on his shoulder, he picked the lamp back up and left the halls. Eureka Springs and a battle waited for him.

TUESDAY, APRIL 8, 1924

"Flushed and decided, he assaults at once; / Explor
His vanity requires no response, / And m
—T.S. Eliot, *"*

Mildred and Phoebe w
tain, heading down to the
even half a day of classes, as   ... had excited
jitters after the game the night   ...ted to look at the new issue
of *Life* magazine and had asked   ...e to walk down to the library with her.

She always enjoyed the trip down the mountain. Carved out of the very rocks, the steps seemed a natural part of the mountainside, and she found the boughs of the elm and oak trees comforting as they arched over the path. Tiny blue flowers bloomed alongside the rocks and filled the air with a pleasant scent. Robins and bluebirds sang among the branches around them as they walked.

"What happened last night on the train, Phoebe?" Mildred stopped on the trail. She used her heel and dug at the edges of one of the rock steps. "Was that supposed to happen?"

The events on the train last night kept her from sleeping soundly. Fatigue had weighed heavily enough on her that she had gone to sleep quickly. Dreams and visions of the horrible creature poised to leap on Phoebe had plagued her not only while she slept, but also during the lessons. She looked all day for a chance to talk to Phoebe alone about the talking board, the shattered windows, and the terrible, ear-breaking screeches but could not find one until now. If last night had shaken her this badly, she couldn't fathom what it had done to Mary.

Phoebe stopped a few steps below her. She lifted her head toward the branches above them and exhaled through tightened lips. "I don't think so."

Mildred held her hands out to her sides. "Well, that makes me feel better about the whole thing." She pulled her arms back in. "Seriously, Phoebe. What did you think would happen?"

Her friend shrugged and worried the hem of her left sleeve. Mildred noticed that Phoebe's fingers quivered. She ran her fingertips across the fabric a couple of times and then swiped the back of her hand across her wrist.

"Not that."

After a few silent moments where Phoebe didn't offer any additional insight, Mildred lowered her voice and leaned down closer to her friend. "Did you see that thing on the top bunk?"

Phoebe tilted her head to one side. "What thing? What are you talking about?"

A cool breeze lifted through the trail, and Mildred rubbed her upper arms with the palms of her hands quickly. "That's why I knocked you down, Phoebe. There was something on the bunk, and I thought it was going to pounce on you."

The wind settled, and the leaves stopped rustling. Phoebe pinched the tip of her nose and squinted at Mildred. "When did you knock me down?"

"On the train?"

"Why did you do that?" The base of Phoebe's neck reddened and started to creep up toward her face. "You could have hurt me."

Mildred curled the left side of her upper lip. "Are you serious? I tried to keep you from getting hurt."

Phoebe put her hands on her hips. "What did it look like?"

"Like a skinny dog with longer back legs than it had front legs." Her friend's contemptuous behavior sparked an anger deep inside her chest that threatened to rise until she would be screaming at the top of her lungs. How dare she think she would knock her over just to cause her harm?

"Did anyone else see it?"

"How could you not have seen it?"

Phoebe pouted. "I guess *I* was too busy trying not to get thrown out of the window."

"Why are you saying this, Phoebe?" Mildred's shoulders slumped, and her arms hung loosely at her side. "We have been best friends for four years."

A fat male robin landed on the trail a few steps below them, and Phoebe watched it hop over to the edge and start to scratch in the undergrowth beside the stone steps. She suddenly turned back to Mildred. "You're right. I'm sorry. I guess I'm tired."

"Okay." Mildred felt confused.

"I didn't see anything on the bunk," Phoebe said. "But if you say it was there, then it was there. Let's go look at your magazine."

They continued down the trail away from the Crescent, alone except for the birds and a lone chipmunk that chattered at them before it scampered away. The steps opened onto Spring Street beside the Crescent Spring, named for the building on the hill above it. As they neared the bottom of the stairs, Phoebe pulled her to a halt and put a finger over her mouth. She pointed down the hill, where Mildred could see Mary sitting on the gray stone wall around the spring. The girl was looking up into the green and yellow painted gazebo, her lips moving as if she spoke to someone in the rafters.

Phoebe motioned for Mildred to follow her. "Be quiet."

"What are you going to do, Phoebe?" Mildred whispered but thought Phoebe did not have anything Mary would like planned.

"Nothing," Phoebe frowned. "I just want to listen."

Mildred sighed and trailed after Phoebe along a ledge above the gazebo. It had rained the day before, so the ground was soft and muffled their steps. Holding the hems of their dresses off the ground, the two girls quietly approached the spot just above the roof.

When they stopped, they could hear Mary's voice plainly. She hadn't been talking to some unseen person in the rafters, only praying.

"What should I do, Lord?" Mildred heard the girl ask. "I think Miss Elise suspects the truth. Do I hide it from her? Graduation is in only two months, and I can leave this miserable place."

Phoebe glanced over at Mildred and arched her eyebrows in a question. Mildred shrugged and listened.

"I pray that you guide me in this difficult time, Father," she continued. "And that you give me the wisdom and the strength to do what it is You would have me do."

She didn't say anything for a long while, and Mildred's thighs ached from bending over in one position for so long. Nodding to Phoebe, she pointed back up the trail, but her friend shook her head back and forth quickly, holding up one finger. Mary continued praying moments later.

"Also, forgive me for not being able to go to confession with Father McHolden the past few weeks. I would not be able to look at him if I told him. I know he is Your instrument on earth, Lord, but I would ask that You forgive me and wash me clean of this sin."

Mildred leaned closer to the ground and could see everything but Mary's head. The girl crossed herself and sniffed as if she had been crying.

"Lord, I ask that You allow J.W. to come to love me, and... to love our child," she said.

Phoebe covered her mouth and gasped, but a car rumbling by on the street beside the gazebo drowned the sound. The two girls scrambled back along the ledge and ran as fast as they could back up the stairs. When they reached the top, Mildred glanced over her shoulder but could not see Mary on the steps behind them. Without waiting any longer, they went back to Phoebe's room.

After Mildred closed the door, Phoebe threw herself on the bed giggling. Mildred frowned at the girl, wondering what she found so humorous about what they had just heard. She opened the door a crack to see if the hall was empty and closed it back, turning to face Phoebe.

"This is serious, Phoebe. It's not something you should be laughing about."

Phoebe sat up on the edge of the bed and nodded. "You're right. I just can't believe it."

The girls looked at each for a moment, then Phoebe asked, "You realize that J.W. is the father, don't you?"

Mildred frowned. "How do you know?"

A thin smile appeared on Phoebe's face. "Because she told him she was a virgin." She chuckled and covered her face with her hands. "You know this means we have to invite her to our little gathering tonight, don't you?"

"Why?"

Frowning, Phoebe replied, "Because I'm going to have J.W. get with her again."

Mildred wrinkled her face in confusion. "But why, Phoebe? This is precisely what got her into the mess."

Her friend smiled. "Remember her prayer? She wants J.W. to love her."

Still not understanding what Phoebe intended, Mildred shook her head. "But if J.W. gets with her again, she'll think he does."

Phoebe nodded quickly. "Precisely."

"I'm lost. After all these years, I still can't understand why you do this."

"Listen, Mildred." Phoebe held her hands out, and Mildred knew she was getting ready to hear a sermon. "How many times do I have to tell you, *sex* does not mean love. It is only the constraints of a masculine-dominated society that says sex is bound by the constraints of marriage for women yet promotes it at any stage of life for men."

Mildred shook her head and frowned. "You've been reading that *Birth Control Review* too much." She walked over and sat on the edge of the bed.

Phoebe glared at her. "Why? Because it's true?"

"No. Because both men *and* women should be bound by marriage."

"You don't seem to have a problem with it when you're with James Dozier," Phoebe waggled a finger at her and raised an eyebrow.

"But we don't do anything but pet and kiss."

"You haven't lain with him?" Phoebe arched her neatly trimmed brows, cocking her head to one side.

Mildred shook her head. "No. That's something I'm saving for marriage."

Phoebe laughed. "I thought you more liberated than that, Mildred. Sex is a beautiful thing that should be enjoyed by women as well as men."

"I don't know, Phoebe. That is what started this whole thing anyway."

"Then don't know," Phoebe's voice was clipped and short. "But don't you say a word to Mary about this, or I'll do my best to make the rest of the year here as hard as possible for you. I might even have my father talk to some of his friends in Washington and make things difficult for your parents."

"Why would you do something like that, Phoebe?" Mildred asked. "I thought we were friends. This is the second time in the last hour that you've acted like I would do something to hurt you."

"We are." Phoebe sat at her vanity and started brushing her hair. "Just don't ruin things for me. When she finds out J.W. doesn't love her, it'll make her remember she's not one of us."

Mildred shrugged. "Fine. But I doubt that you'll ever let her forget that."

"And she shouldn't." Phoebe set the brush on the vanity and swiveled around to face Mildred. "Both her parents were immigrants, dear. She's not even American."

"I thought your great-grandparents came over from Scotland?" Mildred threw herself back onto the bed, looking up at the ceiling as she let out a huff of air.

She heard the sneer in Phoebe's voice. "You know what I mean. Her parents weren't born here."

"Fine." Mildred picked herself up off the bed. "I just get tired of these petty little games."

Phoebe narrowed her eyes at Mildred. "Why don't you just go get ready?"

Mildred turned and grabbed the doorknob. "And don't forget what I told you," she heard Phoebe call after her.

Phoebe knocked on Mary's door and waited for the girl to answer. She quickly looked around the hall to make sure no one would know she had talked to Mary, but it was empty. After what seemed like a full minute, Phoebe heard someone move around the room and shuffle toward the door.

It opened a crack, and Mary peered out, her eyes puffy and red. When she looked up, Phoebe smiled the most sincere smile she could. Mary frowned, wrinkling her forehead and pursing her lips. She looked behind Phoebe before opening the door wider.

Phoebe stepped in and looked around as Mary shut the door behind them. Her plain white counterpane lay rumpled on the bed, as if Mary had been lying down or napping. One of the closet doors stood slightly ajar, enough for Phoebe to see that Mary had only four dresses besides the required white Peter Thompson.

Mary walked over to shove the door closed. She turned and glared at Phoebe. "What do you want?" Her lips were drawn tight and her eyes narrowed to slits.

Whirling around, Phoebe walked over to the corner of the vanity. She looked at Mary and smiled. The late afternoon sun shone through the open window and cast a pale golden circle on the floor at Mary's feet. The mauve satin curtains ruffled slightly in the breeze and a scent of talcum powder hung in the room.

"I just wanted to invite you to our little petting tonight." She picked up Mary's brush and turned it over in her hand.

Mary looked around suddenly, then back at Phoebe. "Why?"

Phoebe shrugged and set the brush down. "Because without you, we would not have won the game last night."

At that, Mary relaxed her shoulders and a tiny smile crept over her face. "Thank you, Phoebe. But Coach Goldman was right…it took the whole team."

Phoebe waved her hand and walked closer to the window to catch some of the breeze. The days were getting warmer, and she knew it would only get even hotter as graduation approached.

"Yeah, but you scored twenty points!" She puffed her cheeks and blew out a quick breath of air. "That is just amazing. You're probably the best basketball player in the country."

Mary reddened at the compliment and looked at the floor, shuffling her feet. "Thank you, Phoebe. But really, I couldn't have done it without you or Mildred."

Phoebe smiled and walked over to Mary, patting her on the shoulder. "You are so very sweet, Mary." She moved over to the door and stopped with her hand on the knob, glancing over her shoulder. "So you'll be there?"

Mary hesitated before answering. "I don't know."

"Oh, come on. All the girls are going to be there, but the Comets get first pick."

Smiling, Mary said, "I guess."

"Good. Then be in Irene's room at ten tonight."

"But Irene is still in Kansas City with her parents." Mary's eyes darted around the room, and Phoebe wondered if she was looking for someone to jump out of the corners and reprimand them.

Phoebe smiled and laughed. She never did like her own shrill giggle but it was appropriate in this situation. "If we don't meet in Irene's room, how do you think we'll get the guys up here then?"

Mary chuckled, nodding. "Okay."

Grinning, Phoebe opened the door as Mary walked over to the bed and jumped onto it. After she closed the door, she squinted her eyes and smiled. She hurried through the hall and bounded down the stairs two at a time until she stepped onto the first floor landing. The sitting room was half filled with several students, and Richard Thompson stood by the fireplace talking with J.W.

She tiptoed around the fireplace to get behind the college president so J.W. could see her. He and Mr. Thompson were discussing where a new shipment of four-by-four beams for the new arbor in the garden would go. Phoebe motioned for J.W. to meet her in that garden after he saw her standing behind Thompson.

"I'll just go take a look, if you don't mind, Mr. Thompson."

The school president nodded and smiled at his suggestion. "Sure. You know where it is."

Phoebe hurried out the front door and turned left toward the garden. Blooming dogwoods with their blood-edged white petals lined the stone path, and purple and red irises along with lilies grew a little ways from the walk on either side. The white lilies stood out from the deep green of their leaves, reaching for the afternoon light.

She stood at the back of the garden and waited for J.W., taking a moment to hold one of the lilies in her hands. The garden, with all its flowers and quiet, had become her favorite place to get away from the humdrum existence of the school since she first came to the college. A toad peaked out from beneath one of the plants and froze. She nudged it with her foot until it hopped back deeper under the foliage. Something so ugly amongst such beauty should always remain hidden.

The confident tread of heavy boots on the stones warned her that someone was coming down the trail. She stepped around the corner of one of the outlying buildings, waiting. J.W. appeared, looking around for her.

She jumped out and startled him, but he recovered quickly and smiled at her as she tumbled into his embrace. He lifted a lock of her hair that had fallen from her hat and kissed her lightly on the cheek.

"What is it, Phoebe?" His eyes roamed over her face.

Phoebe looked up at him from beneath her blinking eyelids. "Do you love me, J.W.? Tell me."

The young man frowned and held her away from him. "Of course, I do, Phoebe. You know that. Why do you ask?"

She ignored the question and pressed on. "Do you love Mary?"

He snorted and hugged her to his chest. "That little breeze of a girl? No. Why? Are you worried about that?"

Phoebe rocked her head back and laughed. "Goodness, no. I just need you to do a favor for me."

"Anything. What is it?"

"I want you to bed Mary tonight."

"Again? Why this time?" J.W. wrinkled his nose and grimaced. "She's not nearly as interesting as you are." He reached for the hem of her dress, but she slapped his hands away.

After looking around the garden, Phoebe leaned closer and quietly told him of her plan. He protested at first, until she informed him that Mary was pregnant with his child. She told him of the prayer Mildred and she had overheard. She went on to tell him that she wanted Mary to think that God had answered her prayers.

"It'll be funny."

J.W. seemed a little confused. "I don't know about this, Phoebe. It doesn't seem right. If she has this baby it could ruin our chances to be together."

Phoebe flinched and made a gagging sound. "Please. Just let her have a bastard. You don't have to claim it."

"Are you sure?"

Phoebe stomped her foot on one of his boots, causing him to pull away from her. She put her hands on her hips and looked at him sternly. "How many times do I have to tell you that sex is just physical and it is not love?"

J.W. grimaced and scratched the top of his head. His shirt stretched where his arm bulged each time his hand moved to the back of his head.

She blinked twice, gathering her thoughts. "If you want to marry me, you had better learn that I am not going to be bound by men's antiquated ways of thinking."

He nodded. "Of course."

"Good. I will not have some daughter of the hired help thinking she's just as good as the rest of us."

"Sure." He grabbed her hand and started to walk down the path.

"Are you crazy?" She pulled her hand free. "If Mr. Thompson catches us, it could ruin everything."

Phoebe ran ahead of him, waving over her shoulder as she came out of the garden and ran up the stairs to the Crescent. She stopped inside the door to determine if anyone had noticed her absence. When she was satisfied that no one paid her any more attention than they should, she strolled down the hall to the stairs, whistling a Bessie Smith tune she had heard on J.W.'s radio the week before.

Pushing her door shut by leaning her back against it, Phoebe barked a quick laugh and covered her mouth with her hand. Her room waited neat and pristine for her as it always should be. Twenty dresses—two of them her mother had bought for her when they summered in Paris last year—hung on the rod in her closet, and the finest ivory combs and brush lay atop her vanity beside a hand mirror gilded with ivory and gold on the edges. Nothing but the best for her, and this little upstart from a couple of immigrants would never stand in her way from the things she wanted.

She walked over to her bureau and pulled the bottom drawer open. After moving aside a cashmere throw, she pulled out the talking board and set it on the floor. With the bed between her and the door, no one would accidently see it should they burst into her room. Just to be safe, she went over and turned the key in the lock before returning to the other side of the bed. She picked the planchette up and ran her hands over the rounded edges. The wood felt cool to her touch, almost cold in spite of the warm day. Even though she knew no one could have sneaked in without her knowing, she glanced around nervously to make sure.

Holding it gingerly in her hands, she set the wood piece gently on the surface of the talking board and took in a deep breath. Her thighs burned from crouching, but her heart fluttered in anticipation. She licked her lips and then let her breath out slowly.

Her thoughts ran wild on her for a moment, chaotic notions raging through her mind as she tried to focus on why she truly wanted to consult the board. Could she ask it if she and J.W. would have children? Would she ever be taken serious in a world dominated by these idiotic brutes that puffed out their chests and roared at the tops of their lungs as if they would be found to be right and just only because they could drown out all their dissenters with their volume? Would she ever be rid of little people like Mary that tried to pry themselves into polite society?

Phoebe closed her eyes and relaxed. The tightness across her shoulders and down her back melted away, and she felt a tingling in the ends of her fingers where it rested on the planchette. She opened her eyes, letting a small grin stretch across her face.

"Who are you?" That is what she truly wanted to know. Did Mildred have anything to worry about? Was that dreadful girl Mary right about nothing good coming from using the talking board?

Steadily, the wood piece spelled out *No one. Every one.*

The tingling in her fingers expanded through her hands. Was the damn thing working? Maybe it wasn't a person at all.

"What are you?" Was this the question that would get her the answers she sought? The thought that some supernatural being could have been guiding her hands sent shivers through her. Never in her life had she allowed other people to control her. Her father had tried, sending her to boarding school in New England. But it didn't work, and she had become even more independent. No person, especially a man who thought only of whiskey, cigars, and mistresses would ever tell her how to behave or with whom she could correspond.

The planchette moved beneath her hands, spelling portentous words. *That which was promised.*

"What does that mean?" She hadn't meant to speak the question aloud, but the piece started moving. She had always prided herself in her memory, and it didn't fail her now.

That which opens the path. Her brother had never told her that the talking board could be so obtuse and difficult to understand. What path? The path for whom? Perhaps this thing or whatever it was would open the path for her to be everything she had always imagined she could be. She was ready for the world, but would the world be ready for her? Many things needed to be changed, and she could not imagine anyone who would be better suited to lead the world to perfection.

She sat down with her knees raised on either side of the board and her hands on the planchette between her legs. "Is this my path?"

Without hesitating, the wooden piece began its spiraling dance, spelling out the answer to her question. *If you choose.*

The answer seemed furtive and timid to her. She wished that the board would be more forthcoming and direct with its responses instead of making it seem as if she needed to interpret and ponder on everything it said. She attempted to be straightforward and honest with her own answers and explanations because it made things much simpler for her when dealing with all those beneath her—she hated to have to repeat herself.

"Will you show me the path?"

She waited as the board answered in laborious circles and sweeps across its face, spelling out the reply. *If you will follow.*

Heat flushed up from her stomach, spreading across her chest and up to her face. If she bothered to look in the mirror, she knew she would see her face colored like a blushing school girl after her first kiss. But nothing could embarrass her now. She knew nothing but opportunity lay before her. But why should she follow? Should she not lead?

"If this path goes where I think it should, I will follow." Phoebe shivered suddenly. If the power behind the board could help her reach her aims, she would follow it anywhere and everywhere. She would wipe out all resistance before her. If she couldn't do it herself, then she would needle, cajole, or manipulate someone or something to do it for her.

She picked up the board and put it back in her bottom drawer, making sure to pull the throw over it so the casual observer would not accidently find it. The last thing she needed was the ignorant school staff finding the talking board. With their Victorian superstitions, she would not be able to explain its power to their simple minds. For now, she had to make arrangements for their little petting party tonight.

With everything straightened and in its place, she left her room and hurried down the stairs to the ground floor. She looked in the salon near the front fireplace but did not see Mildred milling about with the five other students. One of the underclassman glanced up and saw Phoebe standing there, her face beaming a wide smile. The girl waved, her hand fluttering back and forth in front of her, but Phoebe ignored her and turned away. She walked down the hall to see if maybe her friend had ambled down to the dining room early.

Only the kitchen staff wandered amongst the tables, setting the dinnerware and utensils and pouring water in the clear glasses above all the plates. The smell of braised veal and fire-roasted corn drifted from the kitchen. Her mouth watered, and she licked her lips. Her stomach growled, so she reached down and put her hand over her waist. A junior cook wheeled out a pastry cart laden with lemon scones and sweet bread. Phoebe walked over to the cart and tore a piece of bread from the plate, tossing it into her mouth. The young cook opened her mouth to protest, but Phoebe just scowled and put her finger over her pursed lips. Shaking her head back and forth and frowning so tightly her brows nearly met above her eyes, the woman waved Phoebe back out the door.

She walked back down the hall, looking quickly into Mr. Thompson's office. The college president had either already left for the day or was out running an errand, but the chair behind his desk sat empty. Not wanting to waste too much more time looking for Mildred, she picked up the hem of her dress and sprinted back up the stairs to the third floor. She knocked on Mildred's door, but no one answered. Further down the hall, Ruth Clayton came out of her room, dressed for dinner. She looked up and down the corridor, nodding and smiling briefly at Phoebe when she saw her. Smirking, she nodded back at the other girl, but twisted around and strode away with long, purposeful steps.

Phoebe hated Ruth almost as much as she did Mary. The girl's family had money—probably more than the Stuarts—but it came from old money in Europe. Her family had not been in the country very long, and she couldn't think Ruth's family was better because the Stuarts had made their money here in America. They had certainly benefited from inheritance down through the years, but each subsequent generation of Stuarts had increased the family's value rather than just living off the shoulders of those that had come before like wealthy Old World families did.

Remembering the smells from the kitchen, she decided to go to her room and change for dinner. She would just have to talk to Mildred later, hoping she could explain to her the importance of not allowing Mary to think she was a part of their group. As she went down the hall, she heard giggling laughter like a bunch of children playing some random game. Looking over the railing, she saw Mildred and Mary huddled together as they came up the stairs. She snorted and stomped away, slamming her door shut after reaching her room.

—

Mary stood and waited with the other girls. Her hands felt sweaty, and she feared they would be too slick to help with the rope. Irene had come up with the idea of letting the young men climb up to her balcony using a rope ladder to get around the "girls only" rule established by the school back when it opened in 1908. After a visit to Chicago with her family, Irene had told them of petting parties. The students were all anxious to participate—after all, many of their parents had married and had children themselves before ever going to college. Irene and Phoebe constantly tried to convince the others that society was due for a revolution, and the right to vote for women was just the start.

Irene was especially fond of quoting Susan B. Anthony every chance she had. Mary could imitate her nasal voice fairly well—which she did when she was alone or angry with the treatment she received from the other girls. "The fact is, women are in chains, and their servitude is all the more debasing because they do not realize it."

Phoebe would often preach on her own that if men had the right to philander around, then woman had just as much right. They could pound each other on the backs for their many accomplishments just as men did.

Mary jumped and nearly dropped the rope when she heard the first whistle. On Phoebe's signal, she dropped the ladder over the balcony edge. It tightened and creaked as someone started to climb it. Wiping her sweaty hands on her dress, her heart started to pound, threatening to burst out of her chest before she had a chance to see J.W.

The young man himself peered over the edge and looked first at Mary, smiling. She swallowed nervously and grinned back sheepishly, losing herself in his blue eyes. Mary couldn't help but notice that Phoebe never once looked at him and seemed anxious to see who would climb up next.

When they had finished, ten different young men crowded into the room with the twelve girls. J.W. stood close to the balcony and looked out at the grounds once before pulling the curtains tight. The twins Frank and Thomas Davidson were both lost in conversation with Phoebe, jostling back and forth for her attention. They were both good looking, but not nearly as handsome as J.W., Mary thought.

"Okay," Phoebe whispered urgently. "Let's hurry up and get started."

Mary met J.W.'s gaze and smiled when he nodded at her. She felt flushed and excited that he even noticed her.

"Mary gets to pick first," Phoebe's voice broke in on her thoughts.

"Why?" asked Ruth, who was a member of the Comets basketball team, but spent every game at the end of the bench. "She got to pick first the last time she came."

Phoebe stomped her foot and glared at her. "Because she won the game for us."

Mary stepped closer and smiled at Phoebe. She walked over to J.W. and grabbed his hand. As they headed to the door, she heard Ruth gasp.

She turned but Phoebe waved them on. "Go and have fun."

Gripping J.W.'s hand tighter in hers, they slipped out and quietly rushed down the hall to her room. Her roommate would have to go somewhere else with her pick tonight, she thought. If only her father had the money Phoebe's parents did, then she would be able to have a private room and not have to share, worrying about loose lips. This was only the second petting party she had participated in, and she was the one who had to leave every time her roommate brought someone in with her for some petting and other mischief.

When they were in her room and she had locked the door, she hugged J.W. tightly, and he returned the embrace. They held each other until her arms began to ache. After she released him, he lowered his head until their lips met.

Mary let her lips part as his tongue pushed against it, searching. She kissed him eagerly, pulling his body back against hers. Comforting heat crept up her neck until she felt certain that her face was as red as dawn.

J.W.'s hands moved from her back until his fingers ran lightly across the hollow of her neck. She shivered in delight, and goose bumps covered her arms with pleasant warmth rather than chills. He paused a moment when he found her locket.

He held it up and studied it for a moment. "This is beautiful."

She only moaned when his hands moved to the buttons of her blouse and began to deftly undo them. She couldn't wait anymore and began to help him with his own clothes, nearly ripping the shirt from his back. He laughed quietly and kissed her again.

They left their clothing on the floor and climbed into the bed together, pulling the covers over them. The room was dim, lit only by the moon that reached down through the window and cast a pale, ivory light across the floor. J.W. ran his hands over her hips and pulled her into another kiss. Mary sighed, giving herself to him and saying a quick prayer of thanks in her heart.

—

Phoebe watched Mary carefully open the door from her hiding place in the room across the hall. The girl peeked out, casting rapid glances up and down the hall. She ducked back in and reappeared, rushing J.W. out the door. He stopped and leaned down to give her a quick, chaste kiss on the forehead. Phoebe felt a momentary flush of jealousy, but reminded herself that it wasn't love.

After Mary closed the door, Phoebe reached out and grabbed J.W. before he got too far away. She dragged him after her into her own room, closing the door quickly behind them. Not giving him a chance to talk, she pressed against him and covered his mouth with a kiss.

"Did you do it?" she asked after she broke the kiss.

J.W. nodded. "Did you go with someone?"

Phoebe smiled and hit him playfully in the shoulder. "I'm in love with you. Does it matter? I'm not your property anyway, am I?"

He shook his head slowly. "I guess not."

"Good." She tugged at his pants. "Can you manage to do it again?"

He answered her with a kiss, pushing her down on the bed behind her and falling on top of her. Phoebe laughed and held his head against her breast. As he fumbled with the laces of her chemise, she hoped that Thomas would be able to keep his mouth shut.

"Wait." She pushed J.W. off and rolled off the bed. Her bare feet hit the floor, and the short Persian rug felt scratchy to her soles.

J.W. rolled over to his back, and with his fingers laced together, put his hands behind his head. "I have all night." Then he frowned and looked up to the right. "Maybe not all night." He grinned at Phoebe.

She watched him for a moment, taking in his thick arms and the sparse covering of dark hair over his chest. His body reminded her of an inverted baseball bat—wide at the top, narrowing as it went down to the part you gripped. Shaking her head to clear it, she went over to her wardrobe and rummaged through the bottom drawer.

"What are you looking for?" J.W. leaned up onto one elbow so he could see over the foot of the bed.

"Here it is." Phoebe grabbed the talking board and held it up, feeling triumphant.

Playing with the edge of the comforter, J.W. knitted his brow. "What is it?"

She skipped across the floor and hopped up onto the bed, landing with her knees beneath her. "A talking board."

"A what?" J.W. asked, his jaw slackening.

A little anger and resentment welled up inside Phoebe, and she snapped at J.W. "A talking board."

"What's it do?"

She jerked her head around and stared at him. Why did she put up with this? He was pretty to look at and pliable enough that she could manipulate him easily, but he continuously vexed her with his ignorance. If her family had not had such deep political connections to his family, she probably never would have been interested in him.

"Whoah." He leaned back and held his hands up in front of him. "Why the hostility, Phoebe?"

"Sorry." She shook her head to free the cobwebs. Putting on a broad smile, she put her hand over his arm. "It is a way to speak to something beyond this world."

J.W. screwed his face up, looking puzzled. "How's it do that?"

"I really don't know." Shrugging, she pulled the planchette up and set it on the plank. She smiled and opened her eyes wide. "But it does. Just watch."

"Okay." He plumped the pillows up behind him and leaned back. "I'm ready. Are there going to be trumpets or drums with this?"

Putting her fingertips at the base, she cleared her mind—just like her brother had told her to do—and imagined a blank slate of gray with no depth and no definition. Her heart slowed, its rhythmic beat pulsing through her. All sound and sense of place faded, as she opened herself.

"What does the future hold for us?" The same question as last night. She hoped for different results.

The planchette started to move in its wide circle. Beside her, J.W. gasped. "What the hell?"

"Quiet." She hissed, her teeth clenched together and brow furrowed.

"Sorry."

The circle tightened until the point ended at the F. Three more circles, and it again spelled *fire*. The same first answer as the previous night.

"Fire?" J.W.'s voice sounded far away and muffled. "What's that mean?"

Phoebe ignored him, not answering and only trying to keep her mind clear and open to the possibilities of answers from the board. The planchette started to move again. Six completed narrowing circles resulted in *misery*.

Dropping her hands to her sides, Phoebe exhaled loudly. "I don't understand it. This isn't what my brother got when he tried it."

J.W. leaned up and exposed her shoulder with a flick of his fingers. He placed a kisses across her bare skin. "If it means being with you tonight, I can handle a little misery."

She shook her head. "You are impossible, J.W." The planchette and board were both warm when she picked them up and carried them back over to her wardrobe. She tossed them into the bottom drawer and closed it.

Looking back at the bed, she sighed when J.W. pulled back the covers and patted the sheets. "Fine. But let's make it quick. I am still exhausted from all the excitement yesterday."

Laughing, she jumped into the bed, and they started helping each other out of the rest of their clothing. She started to relax and enjoy the moment. Why shouldn't she? Men told stories about it to each other. Why did women have to treat it like a duty to please the man? She remembered hiding in her father's study once, just before starting high school, and hearing the man laugh and boast about conquests and partners. When she asked her mother about it, she had been told to never talk about it, and that the men would be men.

After J.W. left, Phoebe lay on her back and watched the ceiling. The moon outside had sunk low, but its beams peeked through wisps of clouds and thin branches, creating little dances and weavings. Thoughts about the last two nights swirled through her mind. She felt like the talking board was trying to tell her something. Was it a warning? Or was it fate? Never in her life could she imagine misery. Her parents were wealthy and powerful politically. She had nothing to worry about. But something nagged at the edges of her imagination.

The window had been left open a tiny bit, and a breeze came up to rustle through the curtains. Phoebe watched the new shadows play against the wall. A fox screeched somewhere outside, but she didn't even flinch. The wind picked up, rustling the curtains away from the window. She smelled the familiar scent of a bull bay magnolia in bloom. The fact that the Crescent gardener could get one to grow on the grounds here in northern Arkansas amazed her as much as it reminded her of home. But the same mothball scent they had sensed on the train overpowered everything else. She rushed to the window, grabbing it and slamming it shut. Then she turned and ran a couple of steps to throw herself on the bed. Shaking, she rolled over and covered her head with her quilt.

She had told Mildred earlier in the day that she didn't remember seeing anything on the bunk, and she hadn't. But what she didn't tell her best friend was that she felt a presence in the compartment with them. Something she knew that had been waiting for her. And there was nothing she could do. If Mildred hadn't knocked her over, she would have welcomed it. It offered control. It promised power. She knew that is why she tried the talking board again tonight. She wanted to see if it was real.

The talking board represented a power that most people couldn't fathom or even begin to understand. It was something she wanted. To be in control of every aspect of her life. To hold control over other people. Men the world over had victimized women for too long. If the opportunity to get the kind of power she needed to turn the advantage to her presented itself, she knew she shouldn't hesitate. But years of being taught to acquiesce to the wishes and demands of men caused her to hesitate and suddenly doubt herself when whatever had come across last night sought to become part of her. Years of training had forced her to shrink away and fight it. But she knew she shouldn't anymore.

WEDNESDAY, APRIL 9, 1924

"April is the cruelest month, breeding / Lilacs out of the dead land, mixing / Memory and desire, stirring / Dull roots with spring rain."
—T.S. Eliot, *"The Waste Land."*

Mary closed her door and went to the closet, pulling her dress off the hanger and laying it across the bed. She hummed while she pulled her camisole over her head. Sitting at the vanity, she had the brush in her hand to pull out the fit of tangles when a soft knock on the door stopped her short.

She walked over, still humming, and pulled the door open to reveal the housemother. Miss Elise's eyes widened, and she pushed her way into the room.

"What are you doing, child?" She shut the door behind her. "You know better than to answer the door in such a state. You should at least have a robe on."

Mary swallowed her tune and glanced around the room, hoping there was no evidence of J.W.'s visit last night before putting on her robe and tying the sash. The housemother walked over to the window before turning to face Mary.

"What can I do for you, Miss Elise?" She never met the housemother's gaze and returned to the vanity.

Elise shook her head. "I have to ask you something."

"Yes?" Mary picked the brush back up and tugged at her hair. The bristles gripped her hair, and she winced as the brush pulled.

The housemother took a deep breath and exhaled loudly. "I'm just going to be forward with you, and I expect you to be honest with me. Do you agree?"

"Yes, ma'am." Mary set the brush down, glancing up at Miss Elise in the mirror. Her stomach twisted in knots, and she grimaced at the needles jabbing into her.

The housemother turned back to the window and began to fidget with the curtains, brushing away imaginary dust and straightening the fabric on the rods. Her gray hair was pulled into a bun on top of her head, and she wore a deep blue, high collared dress. The soft smell of fresh powder lingered in the air from when she had walked past. Miss Elise never looked disheveled or unprepared for the day from the moment Mary had first started at the school. She couldn't imagine how the woman managed to do it when she herself could barely get her unruly hair to keep from flying away in all directions or couldn't find the right amount of blush to apply.

"How many days late are you?" Miss Elise asked. She put her hands on her hips and frowned.

Mary gasped and grabbed the corners of the vanity. She swallowed, and her eyes widened with fear. Her heart beat rapidly, and she felt certain it would burst from her chest. Bile climbed up her throat and made her mouth taste sour.

"What do you mean, Miss Elise?" She covered the sudden shaking in her hands by opening the side drawers like she wanted to find something.

The housemother shook her head back and forth slowly. "Don't banter words with me, child. You heard my question."

Mary sat up and took a deep breath. "A little over a week," she replied. The lie tasted bitter in the back of her throat, and she clenched her right hand into a tight fist pushing it into her stomach as a wave of nausea swept over her. Pursing her lips, she let out a long breath and focused her thoughts. "Why?"

"You're not pregnant, are you?"

Mary opened and closed her mouth in protest. "Why would you ask me something like that?"

"I know all about my girls." Miss Elise lowered her head and let out a long, tremulous sigh. "Plus, Father McHolden told me you haven't been to Mass for three weeks."

"It's nothing, ma'am." Her stomach tightened even more, and she wanted nothing more than to double over from the pain. But she swallowed a couple of times, and forced a smile onto her face. "I've just been worried with the game and everything. I'm sure I'll start any day."

Elise walked over and put her arm around Mary's shoulder. "Child, I have borne six children, and I know the morning sickness well."

"It was just nervousness." Mary wanted to protest her innocence, but she also needed to get the housemother out so she could gather her wits. "I didn't throw up all day yesterday, and I feel fine today."

"Morning sickness isn't an all the time thing, Mary Elizabeth." Miss Elise gave her shoulder a squeeze. "I just worry about you, child. What would the college think of me if I couldn't keep my girls in line and out of trouble? I would most certainly be let go. You wouldn't want that, would you?"

Mary shook her head. She could feel sweat beginning to form across her brow and between her shoulder blades. "I was just nervous, Miss Elise. I'm sure I'll start any day now."

Elise pulled her into a quick hug, and then walked over to the door. Mary breathed a silent sigh of relief. As she turned the knob, the housemother looked over her shoulder. "You might want to warn Miss Phoebe that Mr. Thompson knows about her visitors."

Mary gasped. She felt her face flush. "What do you mean?"

Elise winked. "You don't think my dear late Harold and I were always with my parents in the parlor, do you?" She left and pulled the door closed behind her.

Mary couldn't believe what the housemother had just said and stood for a long minute looking at the door. The sweet woman would surely be ruined if anybody found out about Mary's indiscretions. She still hadn't thought of a way to tell her father. Last night had been a start, and maybe she would be able to tell J.W. and they could marry soon.

The oldest elm on the Crescent grounds reached high enough Mary could see the topmost branches through the window in her literature class on the third floor. She had read Robert Frost's "The Road Not Taken" many times, committing it to memory long ago. But her mind wandered to last night and the way J.W. kissed her and the way she felt when they made love.

No poem or novel could make her feel the joy she tasted with J.W. The touch of his hands on her throat burned themselves there, and she remembered the shivers that wracked her body after they made love the second time last night. She felt God had heard her plea and had answered by sending J.W. to her bed. Surely, He had his hand in it. Even though she knew in the deepest part of her heart God would not condone their behavior, she held on to the idea he loved her.

It surprised Mary when the other students got up from their desks and started to file out of the classroom, and she looked around in a panic. The muscles in her lower back twitched, making her wince, and she blinked several times to clear her head. Everyone also had all their books and pads with them. Mary looked around and saw even Mr. Larson had cleaned up his desk before heading toward the door.

She reached out and grabbed Mildred's arm. "What's going on?"

Mildred leaned over to nudge Mary's shoulder. "We're going to Lake Lucerne."

"What for?"

Mildred laughed. "You didn't hear a thing, did you?" Mary shook her head, and she continued, "They're letting classes out early for the celebration."

Turning around and looking at the students clearing the room, Mary felt confused. Her daydreaming meant she must have missed half the lesson. "What celebration?"

"For winning the first ever Southern Basketball Championship for the school." Mildred smiled. "Why, I even bet that you're going to be the guest of honor."

Mary fumbled picking up her books. Her thick literature text toppled to the floor. "Why would they do that?"

Mildred bent over and picked the book up for her. "Because you hit the winning shot."

Mary watched Mildred leave and trotted after her, not wanting to be left behind. She hurried to her room and changed into a blue skirt and a white blouse. Her roommate had already changed and left by the time she returned from class. After rushing around, she hurried down the stairs two at a time with her skirt lifted to her knees but was still the last student to climb onto the bus before the driver closed the doors and pulled away.

—

Mr. Thompson had hired a fourteen-piece orchestra from Fayetteville to play in the hall at the east end of the lake above the dam. Several lanterns hung from the trees along the north bank where everyone gathered to listen as the president of the college gave a speech from the floating dock in the middle of the lake. The flames glinted off the brass instruments like sparkles. Down in the valley with the forested sides reaching high above them, the light started to fade and dim toward evening.

He took off his jacket and put it around the back of one of the chairs and looked out at the crowd. Phoebe stayed at the edge of the gathering, looking around for J.W., and barely heard the president as he congratulated the Comets for their championship—the first one in the history of the Crescent College. The crowd applauded, and several of the nearby townspeople complimented Phoebe on her contribution to the victory.

She nodded and thanked them, but kept an eye open for J.W. He had said that he would be here, and she needed to talk to him. She needed to get to him and talk to him privately before Mary could latch onto him. For now, a crowd of people wanting to shake her hand and pat her on the back surrounded Mary. Phoebe realized that the girl wouldn't be able to detach herself from the pack for some time without being rude.

Something wanted to crawl up the back of her throat every time Phoebe thought of Mary. How could such a nobody be the hero of the day? She swallowed a small bit of bile and shivered.

Even the mayor Claude Fuller had joined the throng surrounding the poor girl, which included Judge DeBoise and Julius Labsap—both members of the school board. Phoebe saw a handsome, middle-aged man being introduced to Mary by Chief Maurice Gaines and wondered who he could be. Just as worry threatened to overwhelm her, she saw J.W.'s tall form stepping out of his duck egg blue Crossley two-seater. His father had brought the car back with him from England for J.W.'s twenty-first birthday. It was one of only one hundred made, and J.W. was very proud of it.

Men and their vanity. Phoebe snorted in disgust. And they have the *nerve* to call our table and mirrors vanities.

She weeded her way through the pressing company, apologizing when the gathering forced her to be more direct than polite, and grabbed his hand. He looked down at her and smiled, giving her hand a squeeze.

"We have to talk." She leaned up and hissed in his ear. "Come on."

Together, they went to the boat docks and put one of the smaller rowboats into the water. As they pulled away from the dock, she saw Mary heading into the dance hall with several city councilors packed around her.

Phoebe knew she would have plenty of time to talk to J.W. without being disturbed and asked him to row to the west end of the lake away from prying ears. The water was still cool in April, but she trailed her hand beside the boat anyway and watched the ripples as they spread across the lake. A few puffy clouds were scattered across the sky and reflected off the surface of the lake. Some of the townspeople had brought their bathing suits and were wading in the shallows, their shouts and cries filled with shivering crescendos. The music from the dance hall drifted over the water, and Phoebe almost wished she could just forget this whole mess and dance through the night until morning.

When they were far enough from the shore, J.W. pulled the oars out of the water and secured them in the boat. He looked at Phoebe, smiling but wrinkling his brows.

"Listen," she began. "We have got to do something about this pregnancy."

J.W. stared at her with a blank expression on his face. "What can we do?"

Phoebe dried her hands on her dress and met J.W.'s stare. "Would your father still give you the lumber you company if he knew you had a bastard running around?"

He shrugged. "Probably not."

"Well, I am not going to marry a pauper." Phoebe splashed at a water strider gliding across the surface. "We have to talk her into ending the pregnancy."

J.W. fidgeted in the boat, causing it to rock gently. "That's illegal."

"Then what do you propose we do?" Her voice snapped loud enough that she took a quick look around to make sure no one paid them any attention. J.W. could irritate her to no end sometime, but there would be plenty of time to train him later.

"I don't know."

"It's like Margaret Sanger says," Phoebe told him. "Every woman has the right to choose motherhood. Do you think Mary wanted to get pregnant?" When he didn't respond, she exhaled loudly and then explained further. "She's a devout little Catholic. They believe in virginity and the sanctity of marriage."

"So do Methodists, Phoebe." The edges of his eyes crinkled, and she thought he looked ready to throw himself into the lake.

"Please, that's just doctrine." She waved her hand around in the air in front of her. "All those pastors fooling around down at the Palace don't seem to follow it."

"Okay." He held his hands up. "When do we talk to her?"

Phoebe looked over at the shore to make sure everyone was busy celebrating. "I'll tell her that you want to talk to us on the north tower balcony at eleven tonight. I'll say that you want us to decide and that you want to be a one woman man."

"Will she come?"

She nodded. "She'll come. She is so hopelessly and romantically in love with you, she would have followed you to Europe in the Great War. When we get up there, you kiss me and then we'll tell her that she has to do it."

"Simple as that?" He looked over her shoulder where people mingled on the shore.

Phoebe nodded. "Yes. Now, get me back to the celebration, and you stay away from Mary until tonight."

J.W. rowed them back to the shore where Phoebe let him help her out of the boat, and then she went to look for Mary. While she wound her way through the crowd toward the dance hall, J.W. returned to his car and left.

The doors to the hall stood open, and the orchestra played a John Philip Sousa number. Several people, including Mary and Mildred with the Davidson twins, whirled about on the dance floor. The man the police chief had introduced to Mary stood to the left of the doors smoking a cigarette.

Phoebe walked over to the man and introduced herself. "Good evening, sir. I'm Phoebe Stuart."

He tipped his brown derby and smiled. "Pleasure. My name is Detective Lionel Peterson."

"Oh." She cooed and smiled. "Eureka's big enough to have its very own detective now. If you'll excuse me, I'm going to go get some punch and dance a little bit." Satisfied that there was no longer someone she didn't know, she turned and walked away.

Phoebe went through the doors and headed for Mary and Mildred. The song ended just as she reached the two couples. Mary looked up and smiled when she saw her.

"Hi, Phoebe." The girl's face was flushed, and she kept looking around at all the people, searching. "Have you come to dance?"

The girl was way too happy. Phoebe rolled her eyes. "Not tonight. I need to talk to you and Mildred alone."

The Davidson twins both bowed to their dance partners and went in search of new ones. Phoebe watched them go, ill-disguised contempt on her face.

"What do you want, Phoebe?" Mildred asked with an edge in her voice.

Phoebe glared at her. "J.W. wants to talk to Mary and me tonight. I thought you would be good as a witness."

Mary strained to see over Phoebe's shoulder, her eyes darting around the dance hall. "Is J.W. here?"

"He just left." Phoebe waved toward the door. "He said he didn't feel like dancing because what he wants to talk to us about has been weighing on him."

"Where?" Mary inquired but still looked around.

"At eleven on the north tower balcony." She suddenly felt even more irritated with Mary. Strange visions of her throttling the girl beneath her popped up in her head, and she barely kept a pleased smile from creeping onto her face.

She stomped off without waiting for an answer from either girl and went outside. She pulled up when she almost ran into the detective, apologizing before going around him. Mayor Fuller and his wife were getting in their Buick SW so Phoebe hurried over and asked them for a ride back to the Crescent.

"Is everything all right, dear?" asked Dorothy.

Phoebe nodded. "Yes, ma'am. I'm just not feeling well."

"That's understandable, Miss Stuart," agreed Mayor Fuller. "These events can be awfully tiresome sometimes. I don't even like doing them myself."

His wife rocked her head back and squeaked a short, shrill laugh. She looked out at Phoebe. "Don't let him fool you, dear. He's a consummate politician and *adores* events like these. Anything to show off and pander to his constituents."

Mayor Fuller chuckled. "Now, Dorothy. It's not always like that."

"I just like to give you a hard time, dear." She patted his right arm just above his elbow.

Phoebe smiled at their banter and climbed into the back seat. Looking out the window as they drove off, she saw both Mildred and Mary watching from the doorway to the dance hall. Detective Peterson nodded at both girls but then looked up at the departing car. She believed without hesitation that their eyes met across the little lake. The policeman had to have been in his thirties, but she felt as if she had gazed into the eyes of a wise grandparent or uncle. The thought made her shiver, and she turned around to watch out the front window as they climbed up the gravel road.

—

After she got back to the Crescent, Phoebe remained hidden away in her room that evening, refusing even to come down for dinner. She sat in front of the mirror. But what she really wanted was to understand the urges she felt welling up inside both her body and mind. So much energy trembled inside her she needed to run down the hall screaming. Only her sense of propriety kept her from doing that very thing. Only her knowledge that she needed to be patient kept her in her room. There would come a time some day when all these trappings could fall away, all these false pretenses that people wore like new skins, shedding them with each relationship only putting them on again when that same situation or relationship reemerged. This world was a lie, and she needed to show everyone that it was.

Every few minutes she looked over at the wardrobe, her eyes wandering down to the bottom drawer. She yearned to pull out the talking board, to commune with and channel the rushing flow of power she felt every time she used it. Something wanted her to open the drawer and hold the plank of wood in her arms.

She had never experienced anything like what she had the last two nights. Each of the lines and grooves on the back of her hand took on new depths when she held them up in front of her. Until she used the spirit board, she never understood how much emptiness truly filled her entire life. When she took the planchette in her hands and felt the electric tingling emanating from her fingertips, up through her arms, and spreading out in a comforting warmth, she knew only it could fill her. It felt like the first time she and her brother had sneaked into their father's liquor cabinet to try some gin. The warmth tasted bitter at first, but soothed and relaxed her as it slid down her throat and spread to the corners of her body.

The spirit board did the same thing to her, only it didn't fade like the gin. It revealed even more emptiness to her. Only the warmth or electric power from the spirit board could fill that void. She knew that now. It had revealed her emptiness, her shallowness. Her enlightenment had only just begun.

Mildred knocked and came in briefly around nine, closing the door as slowly and deliberately as she could. Phoebe never said a word to her and only sat there at the vanity. "What's going on, Phoebe? What is happening to you?"

Her friend tried to get her to talk, but Phoebe knew she wouldn't understand. She needed to commune with the spirit board once more before she met the others on the tower. Mildred finally left when Phoebe refused to answer and wouldn't even look at her.

As soon as the door closed behind Mildred, Phoebe rushed over and locked it. The last thing she needed would be for someone to come in and interrupt her work. She ought to be filled. Holes had been revealed inside her, and only the spirit board could fill them. And she needed Mary out of her life. That girl had caused nothing but trouble since she enrolled this year. She and Mildred had led the college for four years. She was about to graduate and step out into the world. This new girl, without even trying, had changed the way things were supposed to be.

Phoebe never minded sharing the roost with Mildred. Before Mary, they had been best friends, inseparable. After this year, Mildred seemed like she didn't need Phoebe's approval any more. Mary needed to be gone. Not only was the baby a problem, the thought of the girl herself ate at her bones.

The next thing she knew, she stood by the wardrobe but had no memory of walking there from the door. She blinked several times and rubbed her forehead above her brows with the butts of her hands.

What was she *doing*? A cough caught itself in her throat, and she nearly gagged, trying to clear her throat. Why was she thinking of these terrible things?

The bottom drawer to the wardrobe had been pulled open. She shook her head, trying to recall opening it. The spirit board lay on top of her clothes, and she had been certain that she had hidden it beneath them.

She knew she couldn't wait. Answers to all her questions lay at her fingertips. She had a hollowness that wanted to be filled.

When lights out came at nine-thirty, she was kneeling on the floor with the bed between her and the door. No one had knocked or tried to bother her before they had to turn in. That was fine with Phoebe because she needed to work out the final details on how she was going to convince Mary that she had to get an abortion. But until then, she craved answers.

She set her fingers on the planchette and cleared her mind. The gray emptiness filled her inner vision and pushed everything away. A tiny ringing rose in her ears, but she focused on the gray nothingness, and it faded from the high pitch to silence. Her fingertips started to tingle, and the hairs on the back of her arms rose, standing on end.

"What does *my* future hold?" Why should she worry about everyone else? She wanted to know her future this time. No one else mattered.

The heart-shaped piece of wood started to move. Her brother had told her that he thought he might have been moving it subconsciously, but she knew certainly that it moved now on its own. The only use she had was to be its conduit, to physically hold it. Where did it come from? Who made it?

After the first series of circles ended, the piece had again spelled out misery. Why? Her name was Phoebe Stuart. She would know no misery. But whatever communed with her from another realm promised her what it said would be true. She felt this with a definite certainty. Then there had to be a cause to any future wretchedness.

She put her fingers back on the wood. "Who is to blame for this misery?"

No electric pulses raced up her through her hands. The piece remained still. Voiceless. Was it because she already knew the answer? Mary. It had to be. Everything had slowly fallen apart since she had come to the school. She had J.W. wrapped around her finger until Mary enrolled. She didn't want it to bother her as much as it obviously did. She wanted to be liberated from emotional dependency on a man. But she couldn't help but to feel a smoldering anger whenever J.W. let his gaze wander to Mary. And he hadn't put up any fight both times she asked him to seduce the girl. Before Mary, J.W. only had eyes for her, so it didn't matter that she had lain with someone else while he was with Mary.

Something had to be done. She would take care of the unwanted baby and the mother both. The wood plank beneath her caught her eye. Two lines of black letters stretched from the left side to the right and below it a line of numbers from zero to nine. On the left side above the top row of letter was etched the word *Yes*. And on the opposite side the word *No*.

Phoebe felt impelled to pick up the piece and ask one more question. "Will you help me rid myself of my problems?"

The jolt burned through her fingers, and a sharp cry escaped her lips. There was no hesitation in the piece's movements. It moved straight and firmly to the single word *Yes*.

A sense of threatening dread suddenly filled Phoebe, and her heart felt heavy and sluggish. Something ghastly was going to happen, and she had a chance to stop it. But she swallowed with difficultly and stamped down the rising sense of trepidation with the calm assurance that whatever she did would be right. She had a reputation and a golden future to preserve, and some servant's daughter would not have the power to ruin her life. She was Phoebe Stuart. All of her life had been laid out in front of her as she had planned.

She looked back down at the plank, silent and menacing. "How?"

The tiniest part of the corner still touched the back of her left forefinger. A shock coursed up through her arm and tore up into her neck like a hot wire had just been ripped out from beneath her skin. Her muscles ached like it did after Coach Goldman put them through the paces, but her mind felt energized like she had just woken up from a peaceful night's sleep.

A gust of wind came through the open window above her, and the curtains billowed out, the edges brushing across her face. Outside in the dark, she heard scratching. She crawled over to the window and looked out. Illuminated by the moon, a grey-skinned creature hung to the eave below the north tower. Its face resembled a long-nosed dog like a German shepherd but with a taut leather hide instead of fur. Its rear haunches were bunched up under it. The thing looked like it could have walked on two legs. Its rear legs were nearly twice as long as its slender forearms which ended in long claws sweeping out and back down like tiny scythes.

Phoebe knew this was what Mildred had seen two nights ago. When the creature pivoted its head around, gray eyes without pupils met and held her gaze. She knew she should be afraid, but she wasn't. Whatever waited on the other side of the curtain and spoke to her through the spirit board had promised to help her. This creature was here to aid her in ridding herself of Mary and the little bastard that grew inside her.

She smiled, feeling a pleasant calm that everything was going to work out as it should settle over her. Her name was Phoebe Stuart. After casting another quick glance at the creature hanging on the side of the Crescent, she ducked back inside and closed the window, latching it securely.

At ten-fifty, she crept out of her room and tiptoed down the hall, wearing only socks in order to walk as silently as possible. She still heard voices in several of the rooms, which was normal after the dances and the girls felt anxious with all the pent-up energy. Phoebe wondered why Mr. Thompson held the dance at the lake—which he owned anyway—rather than in the ballroom here at the Crescent as it usually was every Wednesday. She imagined he just wanted to show off his wealth to the new detective and establish who was in charge.

A dim light burned at the bottom edge of the door to Mary's room, bleeding into the hall, but it flashed out as soon as she tapped on the door. She waited for several seconds until Mary unlocked the door and peered out through the crack. Phoebe smiled at the girl, and she opened it wider. Mildred sat on the girl's bed with her roommate Francis Williams—a girl even more timid than Mary, if that were possible—but it didn't surprise Phoebe to see her.

Motioning with her right hand, she turned back into the hall and waited for the two to catch up. She didn't have to wait long before they were all three headed to the north stairwell. Phoebe noticed that Mary wore a gray skirt with a white blouse unbuttoned at the top and shook her head.

Not a chance. She snorted and nearly tripped over the edge of the bottom stair.

Mary reached out her hand to steady Phoebe by holding her upper arm. "What's wrong, Phoebe? Are you okay?"

Phoebe shrugged her hand off but flashed her a quick, tight-lipped smile. "I just want to get up there and go back to bed."

"Do you know what he wants to talk to us about?" Mary's eyes were wide and her cheeks flushed as they walked up the stairs.

"No," she snapped, but immediately apologized when she saw the hurt look on the girl's face. "I'm sorry, Mary. No, I don't know. I'm just not feeling well."

Mildred walked silently a couple of paces behind them. Phoebe could feel her eyes on the back of her head, but Mildred glanced away every time she turned around. Her best friend had been acting strange lately, and Phoebe just hoped that this didn't mess things up between them. She only wanted to return things to how they had been before. Surely, Mildred would understand after she took care of everything.

By the time they reached the balcony, Mildred had climbed in silence after Phoebe couldn't—or wouldn't—answer Mary's questions. The waning moon hung over East Mountain and beamed down on the balcony. Far below them, a mist had started to creep up and envelope the grounds in a gray blanket. The silver light from the moon made the night seem like something from a dream or a children's book.

Mildred's legs had started to ache by the time they scaled the steps up to the platform. Her chest was tight, and her lungs felt as if she had been playing basketball all evening. She hated these games Phoebe always played, lording her parents' money and position over everyone as if she were as powerful as they. Her eyes hung heavy, and she really just wanted to get back to her room and fall asleep. J.W. stood leaning against the railing on the far side, his slender frame relaxed. He lifted his arm, and Mary's smile slowly faded from her face as Phoebe ran across the landing and grabbed J.W.'s outstretched hand.

Mildred watched helplessly as Mary's face twisted between outright rage and despair. Phoebe whirled under his arm and came to rest with her back against his chest, smiling back at Mary. He leaned his head down and kissed Phoebe on the top of her head, then he looked back across at Mary, who held her arms wrapped tight around her chest as if she were cold.

"I know you're pregnant." He wrinkled his brow, looking directly at Mary. "I'm sorry."

Mildred huffed in disgust and turned to leave, but Phoebe stopped her with a shout. "Wait, Mildred. You have to know that she made this decision on her own."

Turning back, Mildred glared at Phoebe and added as much venom in her voice as she thought she could. "What decision?"

Phoebe prodded J.W. in the side with her elbow. He looked from Mildred and back to Mary. The wind had picked up, swirling up from the gardens below them and carrying the scent of blooming flowers and grass that had been cut that same day.

"You have to get an abortion." His voice was steady, but the muscles in his jaw clenched.

Mary cried out in anguish, and her knees buckled onto the floor. Mildred rushed over and put her arms around the girl's shoulders. She helped her back up to her feet, brushing her hair away from her eyes with one hand and holding her around the shoulder with the other.

J.W. let go of Phoebe and stepped near, but Mary cringed back against Mildred, trying to get away from him. He attempted again to get closer to her, but Mildred held up her hand and pushed it against his chest, shaking her head.

"Listen, Mary." The flatness in his voice was gone, and the corners of his eyes were drawn and narrow. "I'm sorry, but what we did was wrong. Phoebe and I are getting married this June."

Mary cried out again and buried her head into Mildred's chest. Her body shook with sobs, and she clenched her fists tight enough that the knuckles turned white like the moonlight.

"Please, Mary," J.W. appealed. "You have to understand."

"Understand what?" She lifted her head and glared at him. Her scream echoed over the grounds, but Mildred doubted anyone would hear above the wind. "That you want to kill our baby so you can be with that witch?"

Phoebe stepped away from the balcony's edge, but J.W. shook his head and motioned for her to stay back. She ignored him and stood behind him, staring at Mary. Mildred could not see any emotion on Phoebe's face. She ignored everything else and just stared at Mary.

"No, Mary," answered J.W. "My parents will not let me marry you. They have already made plans with Phoebe's parents. I will buy you a train ticket to Little Rock or Kansas City and even pay for the procedure."

Mildred glared at him. "That's very noble of you." She hoped he could understand the sarcastic sneer.

"You stay out of this, Mildred." He pointed a finger at her and snarled. "This is between Mary and me."

Mary looked up with red, swollen eyes, her face streaked with tears. "If I do this for you, I have nothing." Her body shook in Mildred's arms. "I will be damned to hell!"

"No, Mary—" J.W. began, but Phoebe's shrill laugh cut him off.

"To hell? For what? Fixing what's wrong?"

Mary stepped away from Mildred, closing the gap between her and Phoebe. She jabbed the air in front of Phoebe with a shaking finger. "For taking a life."

"It's a condition that can be repaired, Mary." Phoebe insisted. She ignored the finger in her face, and tilted her head to one side, smiling. "J.W. will even pay for it. You can't afford it. You can't even afford to keep it. Besides, it can't even be considered alive yet."

"Oh, please, Phoebe." Mildred tried to stand between Mary and the other girl. "You know this is what she believes."

"I would rather die than kill our baby!" Mary lunged at J.W., scratching his face with her nails. "I am not going to have an abortion, and you are going to marry me. This is your child, and I have never been with anyone else."

J.W. held her hands away from him and shook his head. "I'm sorry, Mary. I can't."

"I love you," Mary cried. "I would rather die."

Phoebe growled. "You little tramp." She stepped forward and shoved the other girl.

Mary stumbled, tripping over the hem of her skirt and fell over the railing. J.W. reached out and grabbed at her flailing form, snagging her locket and keeping her from tumbling off the balcony to the garden. One of Mary's feet found a toehold on the other side of the railing, while the other one swung away from the ledge.

"Please, Mary," he begged, holding her locket but not pulling her back.

"Get her in!" Mildred screamed and ran to the railing, but Phoebe stepped in front of her.

"My parents will not let me marry a Catholic, Mary." J.W. ignored Mildred. "You have to get the abortion."

"I would rather die." Mary looked over her shoulder at the ground far below. The moonlight glistened off the tears streaming down her face.

Phoebe whirled and shouted. "That can still happen."

J.W. turned and looked at his fiancé, his face wrinkled in confusion. Mildred screamed as she saw something snake out from beneath the eave and grab Mary's thrashing foot. She tried to push her way past Phoebe, but she pulled her to the ground.

"Stay out of this." Phoebe's moist breath hissed in her ear, feeling warm against her skin.

With Phoebe lying on top of her, Mildred looked up and saw the clawed hand start to smoke where it grabbed Mary. A piercing screech—Mildred remembered it from the train—erupted over the tower balcony. J.W. screwed up the corners of his mouth, his face wincing.

His hand twitched, and the chain snapped. For a frozen moment, Mary looked stunned then started screaming as she tumbled back into empty space. J.W. leapt toward the edge but missed her flailing arms.

Mildred heard the body strike the stone walkway in the garden below, smacking like a hammer swung against the side of a house. Mary's scream cut off abruptly. J.W. helped Phoebe to her feet, and Mildred quickly pushed herself off the floor. She glared at the other two, afraid to move or even say anything. She wanted to run screaming from the balcony, but something climbed up over the side of the roof and sat on its haunches beside Phoebe.

Mildred watched with wide eyes as J.W. just blinked a couple of times and looked at Phoebe. He jumped back, still clutching Mary's locket in his hand. "Shit, Phoebe. Get away. What is that?"

Phoebe smiled. "Don't worry, honey. It's here to help us get rid of this problem." She glanced over at Mildred. "Is there going to be a problem?"

Mildred shook her head side-to-side quickly. Her mind raced, and she ran through any of the options she could think of to get out of the situation alive. She had just witnessed something horrible. Something she didn't even know if she could believe. The creature beside Phoebe sat on its haunches, and she recognized it as the one that had been on the train two nights ago. It waited next to Phoebe like a pet dog but watched Mildred and J.W. with gray eyes that had no pupils. J.W. stepped toward Phoebe, his muscles tense like he was going to try to grab her.

But Phoebe shook her head. "It won't hurt me, silly. It wants to help." The creature growled, stepping around J.W. and toward Mildred.

She looked over at J.W. and saw Mary's locket hanging loosely in his hand. She remembered how the creature's hand had smoked and it had cried out in pain when it grabbed Mary's leg. Without warning, Mildred snaked her hand through the air and snatched the locket from J.W.

The creature hissed and slunk back to Phoebe, who reached out and stroked its head. She narrowed her eyes and looked straight at Mildred. "You keep that hidden."

J.W. still hadn't moved. His hand was up as if he still held the locket, and his eyes never left Phoebe's side. He swallowed and grimaced. "What is that thing?"

Phoebe ignored him. "Did you hear me, Mildred? You keep that hidden."

"Or what, Phoebe?" Mildred looked at the thing beside Phoebe. "You'll have your witch dog kill me like it did Mary?"

Shaking her head, Phoebe walked over and put her finger against Mildred's chest. "You do it and keep quiet, or I will have your parents and little brother killed. How would you like that?"

Mildred sniffed, sucking in a deep breath. "You wouldn't."

"Try me." Phoebe shrugged and turned back to J.W. "Listen, you two. Just do what I say." She wagged her finger back and forth at both of them. "I will not go down for this. You will both keep your mouths shut and agree with what I say."

She turned and started to walk to the stairs, and the hideous creature slinked back over the side of the roof. J.W. silently followed her off the balcony. Mildred waited for a few moments, looking at the railing, and started to cry.

By the time she made it to the ground, several members of the faculty and students had already gathered in the garden. Miss Elise tried to keep the students back, while Mr. Thompson knelt over Mary's body. She had fallen through one of the blooming dogwoods. Three white petals rested on her chest, and one had fallen on her hair as it lay around her like a golden halo. The housemother had brought a lamp that cast long fingers of shadow and light to weave amidst the trees and shrubs.

Mildred looked at Mary, letting the tears fall freely down her face. Blood soaked through Mary's hair and the petals—once pure white—now blossomed redder and redder with each moment as they absorbed the blood. Mildred heard Phoebe's voice, muffled as if she spoke from inside a hollow bell. Mr. Thompson called her name, but she just looked at Mary's body. The girl, so alive and full of laughter earlier in the evening, lay silent among the dogwoods and irises in the garden, a crushed lily peeking from beneath her backwards-bent arm.

"Mildred." Mr. Thompson's shout jerked her head around. She searched for the man but all the faces looked strange to her.

"Are you okay?" He came up and put his hands on her shoulders.

Mildred shook her head, tears streaking down her face. The housemother came up and put a shawl over her shoulders, helping her back down the path and into the Crescent.

"Poor child." Elise looked over her shoulder at Mr. Thompson. "She's probably in shock."

The president nodded. "Get her to her room. Phoebe, you go with her. I want you both back in bed." He paused for a moment. "J.W., as for you, you know better than hanging around the school. I don't care if you are engaged to one of our students. Get home."

As Mildred let Miss Elise lead her up the steps, the darkness seemed to envelop everything—the voices, the wind, the light—and all was quiet. She didn't realize that the housemother had helped her into bed until the woman had turned out the light and pulled the door closed. She lay there looking at the ceiling, watching the shadows cast by the lanterns down in the garden. Muffled voices drifted to her, but she couldn't even tell which person spoke them.

Sleep had almost finally caught her up when she heard her doorknob rattle. Rising onto one elbow, she watched as Phoebe opened the door. She took a quick glance down the hall before stepping into the room and closing the door slowly so it didn't make any more noise than a small click as it latched. In four quick steps, Phoebe reached the bed and sat down on the edge. Her hand rested on Mildred's arm where it lay above the quilted blanket on her chest.

"Are you okay?" Phoebe's whisper sounded like a harsh hiss in the dark.

It sounded to Mildred as if Phoebe was more concerned about herself than she actually was about her friend. The girl always thought of herself first. Mildred couldn't imagine Phoebe worrying about anyone or anything else in the world.

She rolled over with her back to Phoebe. "I'm tired. Let's just get some sleep."

"Okay," Phoebe said. "Just remember that we're all in this together."

Mildred nodded without saying a word. She couldn't trust her voice, and her mouth felt like dry paper had wrapped itself around her tongue. Her heart pounded so hard she could hear its rhythmic beat through her pillow.

"Sleep tight, Mildred."

The weight lifted off her mattress, and she sighed when her room door closed. Fear raised sweat on the back of her neck, but she still shivered, her teeth chattering. One by one, the lanterns in the garden either faded slowly away or were extinguished. The shadows on her ceiling deepened until the muted light from the moon was the only illumination coming from her window. Everyone must have finally left the garden, and only silence remained. A mist had risen up the mountain, and she wondered why when the moon shown through fog, it seemed to make the night brighter instead of dimmer.

What a terribly mundane thing to think about at a time like this. Trembles started in her hands and reached up into her shoulders. She clasped her hands together, tighter and tighter so she felt an ache across her knuckles.

She thought she would have to wait a long time for sleep. Phoebe's late night visit plagued her with dread, fear, and anger all mashed together like a furious cocktail of bitterness that threatened to boil over and explode. But she had no more thought about the trouble she was in when she closed her eyes and drifted back to sleep.

THURSDAY, APRIL 10, 1924

"After the event / He wept. He promised 'a new start.' / I made no comment."
—T.S. Eliot, *"The Waste Land."*

Mildred stared at the wall behind Mr. Larson. She heard his voice like the distant rumble of a train but couldn't understand what he was saying. Getting up in the morning had taken more effort than usual. With the housemother's careful prodding, she dressed herself, but didn't brush her hair one hundred strokes like she usually did. She felt drained and alone, and the darkness continued to crush her.

Phoebe, on the other hand, looked as perfect this morning as she did every morning. Every strand of red hair lay in its proper place. Every stitch of clothing matched. Every accessory accented her from head to toe, bringing out the green of her eyes and the fire of her hair and the ivory smoothness of her skin.

Mr. Larson droned on about Robert Frost and Ezra Pound and the many contributions they had made to contemporary poetry. This morning though, Mildred couldn't have cared.

"Mildred!" Phoebe shouted in her ear, making her jerk out of her thoughts. She glared at the other girl.

When Mildred finally looked at her, Phoebe motioned behind her to the door where the school president waited. "Mr. Thompson wants to see us."

They walked out of the classroom, wandering between the desks and curious glances, and followed the president down the stairs. He led them to the music room, which overlooked the garden with its stone walkway and all its spring flowers. A man in a single-breasted brown suit and crisp white shirt with a black tie waited by the far window, staring out at the plants and trees as the two girls filed in behind Mr. Thompson.

"This is Detective Peterson of the Eureka Springs Police Department." Mr. Thompson motioned toward the man. "Detective, this is Phoebe Stuart and Mildred Thorton. I will return in fifteen minutes."

Peterson nodded and continued gazing out the window. Mildred looked over at Phoebe, who had a deceptively innocent smile on her face. She glanced back at the detective, but he seemed like he was studying the branches of every single tree in the garden and perhaps those beyond the grounds of the school as well. The two girls waited in silence for five minutes before Phoebe started smoothing her dress against her legs.

Turning around, Peterson looked at them as if seeing them for the first time. His eyes moved across the girls, searching their faces. He nodded and waved to three chairs in the middle of the room. Mildred and Phoebe walked over and sat down. When they looked around to see if the detective followed, they saw he had returned to his perusal of the garden.

Mildred glanced over at her friend nervously, furrowing her brows into a deep frown, but Phoebe looked at her sternly with her right forefinger to her mouth. She arched one eyebrow, questioningly, and Mildred nodded once. Mildred fumbled with the ties of her dress for another five minutes before Peterson exhaled loudly and walked over casually to sit in the empty chair facing them.

The detective opened his mouth to speak, but Phoebe interrupted the man. "How long is this going to take, Detective? We both have studies to attend to if we are to graduate with Science Diplomas next month."

Peterson nodded and pulled a tablet and pencil out of his left jacket pocket. He looked up at Phoebe and scratched the underside of his chin with the end of the pencil.

"I understand that, Miss Stuart," he replied. "But one of your classmates has just had her young life come to a tragic end. I would think that you would be willing to answer a few questions to help us all get on."

Phoebe nodded. "I understand, sir. And as tragic as that event is and with the melancholy that it brings to the college, we all still have lives that must go forward."

Peterson bit his top lip and nodded, then looked at Mildred. "Since Miss Stuart is so willing to talk, we'll make her wait her turn. What happened?"

Stunned by the detective's nonchalant attitude, Mildred sat blinking a few times before she found her voice. After having been drilled by Phoebe for so long during lunch, she knew what to say like a script. "I wasn't really paying attention."

"But what did you see?" the detective asked.

She sucked in a quick breath and looked up to the left, squinting her eyes. "J.W. and Phoebe told Mary that they were getting married in June—"

Detective Peterson held up his hand, interrupting Mildred's recollection. He turned to Phoebe. "Congratulations." She only nodded, and the detective turned back to Mildred. "I'm sorry, Miss Thorton. Please, continue."

"They told her they were getting married and that J.W. didn't love her." Mildred felt her heart pound inside her chest and took a deep breath to calm herself. "Then I heard J.W. gasp and looked up. Mary was gone."

Tears filled the corners of her eyes and began to tumble down her cheek. She kept her hands in her lap and felt a couple of beads drop onto the back of her hand. Detective Peterson grabbed a handkerchief from inside his coat pocket and handed it to her. Holding it spread across her hands, she looked at the plain white cloth.

"Thank you." Mildred dabbed her eyes and then wadded it up tightly in her hands on her lap.

Shrugging, Detective Peterson turned to Phoebe. He held the pencil in his hand, poised over the blank tablet. "And you Miss Stuart? What did you see?"

Phoebe proceeded to tell the whole story. She related to the detective how J.W. and she had informed Mary that they knew of her love for him. They had asked her up to the tower to be able to tell her in private that they were engaged to be married. They also wanted to ask her to quit pining after J.W., because he had made his choice and that she should honor that. During Phoebe's story, Mildred noticed that the detective only held the pencil but never actually wrote anything down on the paper.

After taking a deep, even breath and smoothing her dress again, Phoebe continued her tale. She told Peterson how Mary had become distraught with grief and was screaming and crying all at the same time. Then, in a fit of rage, she threw herself off the balcony. Peterson glanced over at Mildred, who could only stare at the man. The left corner of her mouth trembled as his gaze bore into her. She fought the urge to suddenly confess to everything.

"Miss Thorton," the detective began, startling her with his deep timber. "Do you know how Mary got all those scratches on her neck?"

She swallowed and shook her head. "The trees?"

Peterson shrugged. "I don't know, but we're looking into it." He stood up, and, after putting the blank pad and pencil in his chair, took out a pack of Lucky Strike cigarettes from his inside jacket pocket. "You may return to your classes now."

As the girls were walking toward the exit, they heard the detective muttering, "I wonder why she was lying face up if she jumped?"

Mildred gave Phoebe a panicked look, but met an icy stare. They quickened their pace and went back upstairs for their next class, stopping by Mr. Larson's class to pick up their books. The empty room waited for them, having let out ten minutes earlier. They grabbed up their texts and turned to leave, finding Detective Peterson standing at the door watching them. They both jumped, and Mildred let out a little shriek. She put her hand over her chest, pinching the crescent moon locket between her thumb and forefinger. The detective nodded at them, his gaze resting on Mildred before stepping out of the way and letting them pass. As they walked down the hallway, she cast a glance over her shoulder. Peterson frowned at the back of Phoebe's head but never met Mildred's gaze.

—

It was three in the afternoon, and Thompson had been notified by the police in Seligman, Missouri that Mary's father, Carmine Bencini, had arrived by train from St. Louis and had hopped in a Yellow-37 cab. Earlier in the day, he had tried to reach Bencini by phone only to learn that he'd already left. He waited with the afternoon sun beating down on him and wished he had left his black jacket in the office. The days were getting warmer and warmer, meaning that graduation and summer were coming fast. Every other year, the mood around the college would have been one of pent-up festiveness. But now everything waited quiet and pensive.

The college had been in an uproar all day, and Thompson had difficulties keeping both the staff and the students in line. With Detective Peterson and other policemen roaming the grounds and halls, the students were either excessively curious or terribly frightened. The housemother had been beside herself just trying to keep her charges heading in the right direction.

The arrival of Mary's father posed a different problem for the administrator. He felt certain that he could handle it with the proper diplomacy and sensitivity, but he still worried. Detective Peterson waited in his office, and Father McHolden sat in the lobby in case Mr. Bencini needed him.

He turned to go back inside and take his jacket off when a cab rounded the corner at Prospect and rumbled to a stop in front of the Crescent. Bencini slowly got out of the car and looked around, stopping to stare up at the building. As the man came around the car, Thompson came down the stairs and held out his hand.

"Hello, Mr. Bencini," Thompson greeted him. "You haven't been up here in a while."

Bencini grabbed the outstretched hand and pumped it twice in a firm handshake. "Good afternoon, Mr. Thompson." He pointed up. "Which one's my baby's room?"

Thompson swallowed and turned around, pointing to a third floor window toward the south end of the building. "I believe it is that one, Mr. Bencini."

"Is she in class, Mr. Thompson?" He looked around as they climbed the stairs. "I would like to let her know I've arrived."

"Please, you may call me Richard." Thompson flashed a wide smile.

He nodded. "Then you must call me Carmine."

"Very well, Carmine," Richard began. "Could you come with me to my office? There is something that we must discuss first."

Carmine stopped on the top step and stared at Richard. "Has my Mary been stubborn again?" His cheeks clenched, and he bit his bottom lip.

Richard shook his head and placed his hand gently on the man's left elbow. "No, Carmine. Please, just come with me."

Frowning, Carmine followed him through the doors and toward his office down the hall. Several of the students in the lobby all watched the two walk by in silence. Richard stopped in front of his office door and allowed Carmine to step in first.

Peterson stood when the door opened and the two men entered. He searched Thompson's face and knew immediately that he had not told Bencini the terrible news. Luckily, Peterson didn't wear a badge, which would have frightened the poor man to no end.

"This is Detective Lionel Peterson," Thompson introduced him. "Lionel, this is Carmine Bencini."

Sticking out his hand, he greeted Bencini before he had a chance to say anything. "I'm glad to meet you, Mr. Bencini."

The man chuckled and replied, shaking the detective's hand, "Call me Carmine. Richard and I have already been through this."

Carmine looked back and forth between the two men during the uncomfortable silence that followed their introductions. He frowned and took the chair that Richard pointed out to him.

"What has my Mary done?" Deep lines worried his forehead as he looked first at Thompson and then at the detective. "Why is a detective here?"

Lionel shook his head. "No, Carmine. Mary has done nothing wrong." He looked to Richard for help and relaxed when the college administrator came over and put a hand on Carmine's shoulder.

"Carmine, there is no comforting way to say this," he began. "I have some terrible news. Mary fell from one of the balconies. She's dead."

The man's shoulders sagged and he wrinkled his brow in confusion. He put his hands on the arms of the chair and started to push himself up but sat back with a huff. His brown eyes stared at a spot on the president's desk, blinking rapidly. "But I just saw her Monday."

"I know, Carmine," Richard said. "It happened only last night."

"How did it happen?" His bottom lip started to quiver, and his eyes glistened as they remained fixed on the desk.

"That is what we are looking into, sir." Lionel leaned over and put his hand on the man's shoulder. "I will let you know as soon as the investigation is complete."

Carmine nodded slowly and started wringing his hands together. "Where is she? Can I see her?"

The door opened, and Father McHolden came into the room. He walked over to Carmine and knelt beside him. He put his arm across the man's back, but Carmine shrugged it off and glared at the young clergyman.

"I don't need a priest." He stood up, looking down at the top of Father McHolden's head, and his voice started to rise. "I need to see my daughter!"

Lionel nodded and rose from the chair as well. "I understand, Carmine. She is at the county morgue in Berryville right now."

"How do I get there?" Carmine looked at the detective, his eyes stern and steady, but his bottom lip still quivered.

"Perhaps it would be best if you were to gather her belongings from her room before we leave." Lionel looked at the school president who only nodded. "I will send a man over to bring her back to the hospital here in town."

Carmine didn't say anything and followed Richard out the door. Father McHolden looked over at the detective.

Shaking his head, he said quietly, "Poor man. She was his only child, and his wife passed away giving birth to her."

Lionel stepped to the door of the office and watched the two men walk down the hall toward the stairs. At that moment, he was glad that he would never have to go through the grief of burying his own child. He turned back inside and pushed the door shut behind him.

"Sit down, Father." The priest looked up, his brow knitted in confusion. He glanced nervously at the door before easing himself into the chair opposite the one the detective had returned to.

"What is it I can help you with, Detective?" Father McHolden reached into his pocket.

Lionel smiled. "How often do you pray the Rosary, Father?"

The priest raised his eyebrows. "What?"

Leaning forward until his elbows rested on his knees, Lionel held his hands in front of him, all the fingertips touching and the palms separated. "This community is in danger."

Father McHolden looked around. "From what?"

"What does Paul tell us about strangers in Hebrews, Father?"

"What?" The priest shuffled his feet and pushed himself deeper into his chair. "I don't understand what this has to do with the tragedy we're facing."

Lionel leaned back and held his arms out wide, palms up. "Do you believe in angels, Father?"

"Um." The priest swallowed, and his eyes shot to the door again. "Yes. Why?"

"What does Paul say about angels?"

Father McHolden looked up for a few seconds, his eyes shifting to the center and back to the left. He lowered his gaze at the detective. "Some have entertained angels unawares."

"Yes." The detective stood and straightened his suit jacket and tie. "We have work to do."

"Are you?" The priest twisted around in the chair. "Are you an angel?"

Lionel reached for the door handle, but didn't grab it. "Me? I'm just here as a detective, Father." He looked back over his shoulder. "But I have it on very good authority that this school and community are under demonic threat."

"I haven't heard anything." The priest stood up. "Wait... Why do I not know this already?"

"Open your eyes and look around, Father. It's always in front of you, but you have to be willing to see."

"See what?"

The detective turned back into the office and took an envelope from his coat pocket, handing it to the priest. "This is from the curator of ancient texts at Saint Peter and Paul's in St. Louis. Please, read it carefully. We have work to do." He grabbed the door and, after pulling it open, walked out.

Elise tapped on Mary's door, letting her hand rest on the brass handle—cold at first, but warming quickly under her touch. She let herself in after no one answered and saw Carmine sitting on the edge of his daughter's bed with all of her belongings packed in the box sitting beside him. With his elbows on his knees and his face buried in his hands, his body shook with sobs. His hair was ruffled and his jacket lay thrown haphazardly on the floor.

The housemother came over and sat beside him, rubbing his back with her left hand. She sang some wordless tune just like she would to any of her charges when they were sick or overtaken with loneliness. Carmine leaned against her, and she held him tightly, smoothing his hair with one hand and letting him cry.

Letting out one last sob, Carmine sat up and ran the back of his right hand over his eyes. He looked at Elise and smiled sadly. His nose and eyes were swollen and red.

"Thank you," he whispered.

Elise only nodded and leaned over to pick his jacket up off the floor. She brushed a few strands of dust off and folded it neatly over the back of the vanity chair. Carmine started to push himself off the bed, but the elderly housemother put her hand on his shoulder and shook her head.

"You don't need to go yet, Mr. Bencini. You take as long as you need."

"Thank you." He stood and started to take his jacket off the chair. "But I need to go see her."

Nodding, Elise patted the bed beside her. "Perhaps you should sit back down, Mr. Bencini. I would like to talk to you. There are some... *things* that you need to know."

Carmine nodded and sat down as Elise took a white, hand-knitted sweater that Mary used to wear around the school during the winter out of the box. She sighed, tears welling up in her eyes and spilling over the edges as she started to refold the sweater.

"I can't seem to stop crying." Her hands shook as she set the sweater on her lap. "I wish that every girl who comes through this school had half the sweetness of your Mary Elizabeth."

Smiling, Carmine looked up at her. "She mentioned you often in her letters. Sometimes she felt like you were her only friend here."

Elise shook her head. "Mary was just innocent. Her heart was too easily hurt."

Carmine laughed and smiled a small, tight grin. "I know. She did not know enough of the world, and that was my fault. I tried to shelter her from all the ugliness."

"But she could be awfully stubborn." Elise smiled. "She said that you told her she got that from her mother."

"She did," Carmine agreed. "But I never should have let her come here."

Elise looked at him curiously. "Why did you send her?" She gasped, holding her hand to her chest. "I'm sorry, Mr. Bencini. I should not have asked that."

He shook his head. "No. Don't worry." He blinked a couple times and turned to look at the window. "Ever since her mother died, I have driven Senator Mitchell and his wife." He held up his left hand and twisted the wedding ring he still wore. "They didn't have children of their own, and often told me they thought of her as an adopted daughter."

"That was sweet." Elise put her hand over her chest. "I wish more people would be as charitable."

He took a deep breath and closed his eyes for a moment. "They said they wanted to do something for us. They felt she needed an education to help her in the world. It's hard being the child of a poor immigrant."

"I can understand that." Elise smiled and put her hand over his. "My parents came over from Greece."

"You said there was something that I should know?" His fingers closed around her hand.

Elise nodded. "Now, don't think bad of her."

Carmine frowned. "I could never think bad of my Mary."

"Good." Elise gripped the man's hand. "Because there wasn't a bad bone in her body. But I think that she was pregnant."

His face twisted in confusion. "How? I mean why?"

"She was two weeks late with her blood." She paused when they heard steps coming down the hall, but then continued after they passed. "She also had the morning sickness last week."

"Who would do this to Mary?"

Elise shrugged. "I do not know for certain, but she was in love with J.W. Floyd. His father owns the Western Lumber Company, but he is engaged to another student."

"Which student?" he asked.

She shook her head and let go of his hand. "I can't tell you that, Mr. Bencini, but I told you his name."

Carmine nodded and stood up, pulling his jacket off the chair and putting it on. "Thank you, Elise. You have been good to my Mary, and for that I am grateful."

"She was a joy." Elise laid the sweater back in the box.

He bent over and picked up the box, heading toward the door. He paused for a moment, holding the door ajar with his hip as he twisted to get the box through the threshold, then went out into the hall. Elise stood and wiped the tears from her face before stepping out and closing the door behind her.

—

With the chaos enveloping the halls and all the students, Mr. Thompson decided to let the classes out early and allowed the girls and staff to gather at St. Elizabeth's for an impromptu memorial for Mary. Detective Peterson knew her father wouldn't be there because he had wanted to hold vigil over her until he could leave the next day. With dinner still a couple of hours away, it looked like the entire school milled about the narrow stone walkways or in the foyer of the small chapel itself.

He nodded at several people, including the mayor and his wife, avoiding conversation and searching for Father McHolden. Lionel found the young priest hunched over in quiet conversation with Mr. Thompson outside the chapel doors. Walking up quietly beside them, he nodded when they glanced over, waiting for them to finish. A bluebird lit in one of the trees beyond the chapel grounds, fluffing its feathers and fanning its wings. It finished grooming itself and twisted its head side to side, looking at the detective with first one eye and then the other.

"Did you need me for something?" Lionel turned and saw the two men. Thompson arched his right eyebrow, waiting for him to answer.

Shaking his head and frowning, the detective waved his hand. "No. Sorry. I actually wanted to talk to Father McHolden real quick, if you don't mind."

"Not at all." Mr. Thompson smiled and nodded once at the priest before turning back into the chapel.

Lionel motioned to the rose garden on the side of the chapel with its well-trimmed and crisp green grass. The two walked over and stood beneath the high wall. Neither said a word, and the detective looked up at the Crescent on the pinnacle of the mountain overshadowing even the church that rested on the side of the hill beneath it.

"What can you need from me, Detective?" The priest sounded nervous, his voice quiet and subdued. A fitting aspect for their surroundings.

After inhaling deeply, soaking in the soft fragrance of the roses that had been blooming for over a week now, Lionel turned around to face the other man. "Do you know the rite of exorcism?"

Father McHolden gasped and stepped back a pace from the detective. "What?"

Holding his hands, Lionel replied, "We don't have time for you to be taken by surprise, Father. Can you perform a Major Exorcism or not?"

The priest nodded but didn't open his mouth. He pulled out a rosary from his right pocket and started fingering the rosewood beads between his fingers.

"Good." The detective put his arm around the man's shoulders and drew him back up the path. "We haven't a moment to waste."

Pulling up and resisting his shepherding, the priest looked at Lionel, his brow creased and eyes narrowed. "Why do we need to perform an exorcism?"

Exhaling loudly, the detective lowered his head after grasping the other man's upper arms in his hands and focused his eyes on the priest's face. "I have been at the memorial since it started. There is a key player not in attendance tonight. Why? She never misses a chance like this to be the center of attention."

Father McHolden looked up, shifting from one side to the other, for a few second. His eyes widened. "Phoebe Stuart."

The detective nodded. "Why isn't she here, Father?"

"I couldn't know."

"Unless I miss my guess about the young woman, she has to be involved in every social event to which she has access. In fact, she very likely tries to be the center of such events."

The priest nodded. "That would describe Miss Stuart to the letter from what I have heard. I don't have much dealing with her myself because she is not a member of my flock."

"That may be, Father. But she needs you now. She needs both of us in order to protect her and the rest of the community."

The young man nodded and followed Lionel out of the garden and up the steps leading out of the chapel grounds to the parking lot above. A black Model T waited for them, and the detective motioned Father McHolden toward the passenger door. They shut the doors, and Lionel stepped on the switch to start the engine.

After it sparked to life and started rumbling, he looked up and grinned. "It is so much easier to get these things running with the starter than it was with that unwieldy hand-crank."

Shrugging and raising his brows, the priest just leaned back in the seat as Lionel put the car into drive and lurched away from the church. They drove down Prospect and went on Pine until they reached a brown three-story home that had stairs leading to doors on the upper floor on the right side. Lionel put the car in park, and the priest followed him up into the apartment at the top of the stairs.

Striking a match, he lit a lamp by the front door. He turned the wick up, and warm light filled the small room. The main room had a couch next to a low table in the center and two plush chairs on either side of a rough-hewn stand that held a cathedral-style radio with its three brass knobs arranged in a flattened triangle on the face.

The light from the lantern did not dispel the shadows from the kitchen beyond the couch, but Lionel took the lantern with him into the bedroom just off the living room, forcing the priest to follow him or be left in darkness. He had only a narrow armoire and a camel-back trunk at the foot of his narrow bed.

Kneeling beside the trunk, he lifted the lantern for Father McHolden to hold. With his hands free, he threw off the blanket draped across it and opened the lid. When he pulled out a light crossbow, the priest jumped back and nearly dropped the lantern but didn't say anything. Lionel reached into the chest and pulled out something wrapped in brown cloth.

He set the package on the bed and motioned for Father McHolden to come closer. Untying the cords at either end, he unwound the cloth, revealing a slender silver sword. The flickering light from the lantern made the swirls in the metal look as if the blade was somehow alive.

The priest gasped. "Who has a sword these days?"

"Or a crossbow?" Lionel asked as he pulled out a leather pouch holding twenty bolts.

"Sure." Father McHolden wrinkled his nose, squinting his eyes in confusion. "I know that Chief Gaines has a Browning Model 1922 pistol. Wouldn't that be better for protection?"

Lionel shook his head. "Father, there are some things for which only Damascus steel forged in the Holy Lands and quarrels blessed by the Holy Father himself will be needed. Bullets are mere needle pricks to the things we will face this night."

Fitting the sword in a scabbard, the detective put his arms through the strap and holding the crossbow in one hand and the pouch with the bolts in the other, he motioned the other man to come with him. Lionel waved at a bag beside the front door.

"Everything you need is in there," he said. "I took the liberty of preparing the equipment."

"What equipment?" He glanced at the ground. "How do you know this?"

Detective Peterson stopped in the middle of the living room. He tilted his head up and exhaled loud enough for him to hear. The stern look on the man's face when he turned back around made the priest suck in a quick gasp of air.

"There is a war going on, Father." He lifted up the sword. "A war for the souls of these people, and it is up to you and me to stop it."

"War?"

Nodding slowly, Lionel spoke in a steady voice soft enough that the priest had to strain to hear. "I could give you a long history lesson, if you would like, Father. But if we're to take the precious time to do that, then Miss Phoebe's soul could already be taken. Do you want that on your record when you stand at the Judgement?"

Father McHolden nodded and bent over to pick up the bag. Its strap bit into his shoulder, and the weight it held made him awkward. He trailed after the detective, blowing out the lantern with a puff of air after they reached the door. Lionel didn't wait and descended the stairs two at a time. The car had just started as the priest climbed into the passenger side, only glancing back once to look at the ancient weapons waiting in the seat.

"Where now?" the priest asked.

"Back to the school."

They made their way back to the Crescent, and the late afternoon sun stood just above the horizon, getting ready to dip beneath it and start the journey into night. Lionel grabbed the weapons and the two walked up the front steps and in through the front door. One of the kitchen employees scurrying by from the stairs to the right on her way back to the kitchens took a quick look before continuing on her way.

Time was the most important ally they had right now, and Lionel hoped the priest could keep up with him as he bounded up the stairs to the third floor. He heard the priest panting behind him, but they both arrived on the landing right after each other. Turning left, he glanced at the doors until he came to Phoebe's room at the back of one of the end halls.

Father McHolden pulled up, the momentum of the heavy bag forcing him to shift his weight. "Wait a minute. How do you know where to go?"

The detective let out a long sigh and glanced back at him without stopping. "The Fallen and their parasites leave a distinctive trail and acrid odor almost like vinegar."

"Oh." He took in a deep breath and hurried to follow after the other man.

He pressed his ear against the wood and listened. Only the sound of his own coursing blood rushed through his hearing. Taking the knuckle of his right hand and keeping his ear to the door, he rapped three times. Something shifted inside the room, sounding almost like the window sash being slid up. He thought he heard muffled and hurried whispers in the room, but they stopped when he knocked again. A few seconds later, the window shut followed by steps walking across the floor.

Just as he stepped away from the threshold, the door opened. Phoebe blinked her eyes a couple of times like she was trying to clear her thoughts or the lights in the hall were too bright. But then her gaze focused on Lionel, and a wide smile split her face and lifted her eyes. Her bright red hair shone in the light coming through the windows. Her skin—ivory, smooth, and unblemished—glowed.

"Well, Detective Peterson. Did you have some more questions for me?" She put one hand on Lionel's chest and pulled the other across her lips, catching the bottom one on her forefinger. "Would you like to come in? Everyone is away at the memorial, I'm afraid." She looked at the pommel sticking above the detective's shoulder. "Is that a sword? Why do you have a sword, Detective?"

Lionel grabbed her hands and held them in front of him. "I smell it in you, Miss Stuart. We're here to help you."

"We?" She pouted her lips and then looked over the detective's shoulder. When she saw Father McHolden, her eyes widened and her brows arched in surprise. She tugged at his grip. "What is this?"

He pushed her into the room, and the priest hurried after him, kicking the door shut behind them with his heel. As Lionel forced Phoebe further into the room, the priest flipped the bag off his shoulder and spilled its contents onto the bed. He picked up the rope and set it across the front of the bed. He took the vial of holy water and placed it on the vanity next to a set of ivory brushes and combs.

"This is very improper, Detective Peterson." She pulled harder against his hold, almost slipping out once before he took a firmer grip. "If you do not leave, I will have to scream."

She opened her mouth and took a deep breath, but Father McHolden came up from behind her and put a strip of cloth in her mouth. He quickly tied it before Lionel forced the young woman over to her bed. The priest hesitated, his eyes darting back and forth between the detective and Phoebe.

"Father!"

The priest shuddered, blinking several times. He looked at Lionel, and then he bent down and took Phoebe's feet in his own hands. Together, the two moved her over to the bed. She kicked and squealed through the gag, her feet coming nearly close enough to hit Lionel in the nose. Father McHolden came around to the head of the bed and grabbed one of her arms.

He wrapped the rope around her wrist a few times and tossed it under the bed to Lionel's feet. The detective reached down, and after pulling Phoebe's other arm out flat against the bed, wound the thick cord around that wrist. The priest slid under the bed where Lionel handed him the coil. The detective went down to the end of the bed to pick up the rope where Father McHolden had thrown it. One foot struck him in the mouth, and he tasted blood. He caught her legs and pressed them flat against the bed and tied the rope to them. When they finished, her arms were stretched out to either side, and her legs were held together and pointed straight down so she resembled a human cross.

Father McHolden walked back over to the vanity and took up the vial. He crossed himself first and then over the other two. Phoebe thrashed against her bonds, but the more she struggled, the firmer the rope held. The priest unstopped the vial and sprinkled them all with the holy water. He knelt down beside the bed and started chanting the Litany of Saints. Suddenly, Phoebe stopped struggling and glared straight at Lionel. Her chest did not move up and down with any breathing, but every few seconds, her eyelids fluttered closed and back open.

The detective picked up the crossbow and pulled the string back until it locked into place. He carefully pulled one of the bolts out of the leather pouch he had retrieved in St. Louis and set it in the barrel. After setting it close to him on the floor, he reached over his shoulder and drew the sword. The weight felt right in his hands, like it always did. But it was a thing he tried not to grow too fond of because it had one purpose—death.

Lionel put his back against the wall opposite the foot of the bed so he could watch the entire room. The door to the hall stood to his right, while the window was on his left. Starting softly at first as if he was afraid that they may be doing something wrong, the detective could tell the priest was feeling more confident. He finished the Litany of Saints and his voice grew stronger and stronger with each line of prayer he spoke over the poor girl.

A sheen of sweat had beaded up across her forehead, and her ivory complexion turned gray like the ash found in a blacksmith's furnace. Veins along her forearms popped out. The tendons and fibers of her muscles strained against the rope. A low keening came from her throat because she could not articulate beyond the gag in her mouth. It hummed just at the edge of his hearing. If he heard it, he knew the familiar or whatever had been in the room with Phoebe before they arrived would be called to it.

He gripped the pommel of the sword tight and then relaxed his hands so they did not cramp up when he needed them most. His shoulders tightened, but he kept them loose by shrugging and moving his upper arms in slow circles. Sweat ran down the small of his back. The temperature in the room dropped enough that he could see his breath waft out in front of him like a morning fire. But he could not feel the chill, only the nervous heat.

Father McHolden's words finally broke through his own concentration. The young priest was doing a magnificent job. They just had to hold on for a little bit.

"Everlasting God and Father of our Lord Jesus Christ, who once and for all consigned that fallen and apostate tyrant to the pits of hell—" A shower of glass exploded from the window, cutting off the priest's prayer.

Lionel shielded his face with his left arm and stepped between the priest and the window, lifting the sword with his other hand. Sitting on the windowsill, a creature that had the body of a hairless greyhound and the head of a gargoyle looked at him with solid gray eyes. Its forelimb joints were turned backwards. Its eyes blinked sideways as it watched him.

The creature moved so fast its image blurred as it leapt straight at Lionel. Long claws reached out to tear his eyes from his head. He ducked under the slash, bringing the edge of the sword down across the beast's shoulder, and rolled into a crouch. A high-pitched scream tore from its throat, causing the mirror to vibrate. Lionel saw smoke drift up from the wound, and the creature curled its lip back to reveal multiple rows of needle-like teeth. A drop of saliva dropped to the floor from its jaw. The carpet smoked and curled back like hair held too close to an open flame.

Instead of waiting for the creature, Lionel launched from the floor. He brought the blade up in a slash that would have cut the beast in half from its hip to its shoulder. But it leapt over him and dragged its claws across the top of his head.

Blood flowed from the wounds, some of it dripping down his left temple and stinging the edge of his eye. But he shook it off and jumped after the creature where it landed between him and the priest.

Instead of attacking Lionel again, it turned around and drove its claws into Father McHolden's abdomen. The priest had resumed his prayers and did not see the attack coming. His scream echoed through the room. Lionel jumped over the priest, twisting in mid-air and driving the tip of the blade into the creature's back. It shrieked. On the bed, Phoebe twitched and thrashed against her bonds. The muscles in her jaw and neck tensed, and her skin looked like it would tear away from her teeth. After landing, Lionel stepped back into motion without waiting for the creature to gather itself, chasing it away from where the priest had slumped against the bed.

The creature looked up when someone pounded on the bedroom door. "Why aren't you at the memorial, Phoebe?" The person knocked even harder. "It's the least you could do. This is all your fault anyway."

Phoebe's bedroom door burst open. Mildred stood in the threshold, her eyes wide and her mouth open. She blinked and closed her mouth. His gaze darted back and forth from Phoebe lashed to the bed and Lionel gripping the sword above his head. "What is going on? What are you doing? What's all that racket?"

Lionel jumped over and picked up the crossbow. He put it to his shoulder, tracking the creature as it turned and leapt straight at Mildred. "Get down! Now!"

The young woman pulled her arms across her chest and sat down hard on the floor. She screeched, her mouth opening wide and eyes clenching shut. Lionel fired the crossbow. The quarrel bit into the creature's shoulder but didn't stop it. It opened its mouth, its jaw stretching wider than Lionel would have thought possible. Saliva dripped from its mouth onto the floor in front of the quivering young woman. The creature grabbed Mildred by the shoulders and started to snap its jaw shut but wrenched back like it had picked up a hot coal, slamming into the wall. Where it had touched her, its hands smoked. Its howling drove a dagger into Lionel's head.

He stumbled, using the crossbow to hold himself up, and rushed toward the door. Glancing between the detective and Phoebe, the creature hissed once and rolled out into the hall. Lionel knelt down beside Mildred but kept a wary eye on the open doorway. The young woman shivered, leaning against the wall and moaning. Tears had fallen onto her dress, darkening the fabric where they had landed. She sniffed but didn't bother to wipe her eyes nor her nose.

The detective tried to piece together what he had just seen, looking for a reason the familiar could not touch Mildred. His eyes rested on the crescent-shaped locket that hung around her neck, lying against her chest. When it had fled, the creature ripped open the top of her dress. Something about the locket drew him, and it was the only thing he could see different about Mildred.

He put his hand on her back, rubbing it. "Come inside with me. I want you away from the door in case that thing comes back."

She looked up from her hands when he stood and shut the door, turning the lock. Streaks covered her face, and her ears were flushed red as if she had been out all day in the sun. Nodding, she slowly climbed to her feet and leaned against his arm as he walked over and set her in the chair at the vanity.

After he helped the young woman, he bent over to check on Father McHolden. When he put his hands on the priest's shoulder, his eyes fluttered open, and he coughed. Lionel pulled a linen shirt from the bureau and pressed it against the wounds. Blood had soaked through his cassock, making the black cloth even darker.

"I'm afraid we are done here, Father." Lionel grimaced when the priest winced from the pressure.

Father McHolden shook his head and grunted, breathing heavily. "I can finish. We *need* to finish."

Lionel leaned over, his face inches from the priest's. "Are you certain? We can't leave this undone. I can finish the exorcism."

"The what?" Mildred gasped behind him. "What are you talking about?"

The detective turned around and looked at the young woman. "We are afraid your friend is the victim of possession. And that fiend was her familiar."

Mildred rocked her head back and forth, squeezing her eyes shut and pinching the bridge of her nose between her hands. Her breath came in short little gasps. "I don't understand."

"Listen," Lionel said, putting a hand on her shoulder. "We don't have time for this. I have to finish the ceremony before that creature can return."

"No." The priest tried to sound forceful, but his objection came out as a rasp.

Lionel checked the rags and the blood had already soaked them through. "You can't last, Gregory."

The priest frowned. "I never told you my first name. How did you know?"

"You look like a Gregory." He glanced down at the priest's wounds. When he reached for the shirt drenched with blood, the priest grabbed his wrist.

"I can do this," Father McHolden insisted. "You have to track that creature down and destroy it before it can do any more harm."

"Okay." Lionel pivoted on the floor and looked at Mildred. "Can you watch over him? Get him anything he needs. This is vitally important."

Mildred's jaw quivered, but after a couple seconds she nodded. "I can."

Together, the two of them helped get the priest over to the side of the bed where he knelt beside it. He nodded and motioned for the detective to go.

Lionel held the other man's hands in his own. "You are a brave man, Gregory. God be with you."

The priest chuckled and coughed, a little blood leaking from the corner of his mouth. "May He be with both of us. You're the one going after that beast." He straightened himself and took a deep breath. "Now go."

Without saying another word, Lionel turned and went to the door. He stopped long enough to grab the crossbow and pouch of bolts before securing the sword in the scabbard on his back. After a quick glance back into the room where the priest's lips moved as he quietly completed the rite, he spun on his foot and ran out of the room.

Out in the hall, he followed a trail of blood down toward the west end of the building. The blood was red just like a human's but deeper, and some of the carpet where it had landed looked as if moths had eaten away at it. He tracked it through the hall and turned left down the west wing. The window at the end had been shattered. Some of the glass had blown back into the hall and lay scattered about the floor like a broken silver mosaic.

He saw a black iron fire escape bolted to the side of the building. Climbing out onto it, he glanced up to the roof first, but then tracked the creature down. The trail turned north to the building adjoining the college. Lionel knew it housed the residential administrative staff as well as some of the teachers and other workers. The building also had a huge laundry facility for the school as well as contracting out to some important city offices. But the worrisome thing was the coal power plant in the basement that heated the water and powered the electricity and machinery of the facility. A broad smokestack reached up through the trees and stood nearly as tall as the Crescent College itself.

If the beast found its way into the furnace, it could wreak all kinds of havoc and destruction down on the community. Lionel wanted to avoid that outcome and bent over to pull the bowstring back. He crossed himself and fitted a quarrel into the barrel. With the crossbow up and his finger beside the trigger, he stalked after the familiar. Inwardly, he hoped Father McHolden was able to hold on long enough to finish the exorcism, but he pushed the thought into the back of his head.

The memorial must have ended because he could hear voices growing clearer as they made the short hike up the hill to the college. He wondered how many people had realized that Father McHolden had not returned. But the detective needed to find the creature before it could hurt anyone else.

He went around the north end of the building and saw that the blood trail went up the side of the power plant. To his left, the sun looked like it rested atop the distant hills, pausing before it dropped beneath the horizon to its nightly slumber. Holding his hand up to shield the light he made out the shape of the beast scaling the side of the chimney. Its long claws bit into the stones, shoving their way into cracks and crevices so it could get a purchase up the side.

Taking a couple of calming, deep breaths, Lionel lifted the crossbow to his shoulder and sighted along the barrel. He considered the wind, blowing gently from the southwest enough that it could probably push the bolt up to the right at the distance he stood from the creature.

His finger quivered as he rested it against the trigger with a gentle touch. Sweat dampened the back of his shirtcollar. The creature had climbed to within ten feet of the top when he squeezed the trigger. The weapon kicked against his shoulder, and the twanging snap of the released bowstring sounded true and solid.

Less than two heartbeats later, the creature arched its back and let out a pained howl that faded quickly like a passing storm moving on in the night. The head of the bolt had pierced its heart. Lionel watched as the beast crumbled to ash drifting down from the sky like a dirty snow. The quarrel hung in space for a brief moment and then tumbled to the ground. It clattered against the stone walkway. He walked over and grabbed it in his hands. He could still feel the warmth of the beast, but it quickly faded by the time he returned it to the leather pouch hanging from his shoulder.

Instead of scaling the side of the building and squeezing back in through the third-story window, he skipped up the steps and into the front. A few people had returned and milled about the lounge, talking about the memorial and how much they were going to miss Mary. He wanted to stop and berate them, telling them that the words were too late if the person was already gone. She had needed to know that she would be missed while she still lived, that she could be loved like anyone else in their world. But he hurried up the steps until he reached Phoebe's room.

He tapped lightly on the doorframe. "It's me, Mildred. It's finished."

The door creaked open enough that the young woman could see him. When she did, she pulled it wide and stepped back into the room. Lionel walked in and did not waste any time shutting and locking it behind him.

Further in the room, laying his head against the bed, Father McHolden rested his hand on Phoebe's arm. Lionel stood at the foot of the bed, just watching and hoping to see the priest's shoulders lift or sink as he breathed. But nothing happened, and he couldn't hear anything other than the wind rushing through the broken window.

He started to walk over when the other man lifted his head and struggled to take a breath. His eyes flickered and opened. They took a while to focus, but when they did, Father McHolden grinned and snorted.

"Did you do it?"

Lionel nodded. "Did you?"

He smiled. "We did."

The detective knelt down beside him, his knee resting where the other man's blood had pooled onto the floor. "You are brave man, Gregory. I am glad to call you my friend."

"I am only entertaining. Just doing my job," he whispered. "But thank you."

He closed his eyes. His chest quivered as he tried to inhale. After a few gasps, his shoulders relaxed, and he exhaled a long, quiet sigh. Lionel waited, but the priest's chest did not rise with another breath. The wind blew in through the wreckage of the window, fluttering the curtains.

—

Mildred watched as Detective Peterson took the other man's hand in his and sat there looking at him. He looked like he was trying to memorize every line and feature of the priest's face. He looked at the man and then glanced up at Phoebe. She appeared to be resting easily, as if nothing untoward had happened, as if she would go on living her life as normal. Father McHolden had asked for nothing and given everything. Yet everything they gave was always for other people like Phoebe. Those who asked for everything and bestowed nothing but sorrow in return. A good life ruined so she could go on destroying other lives.

She heard a voice but couldn't tell what it was saying. Shaking her head and blinking, she looked over at the detective. "I'm sorry?"

He smiled softly at her. "I was just asking if we could move her to your room."

"Why?" Mildred frowned. When the man looked back at Father McHolden, she gasped. "Oh. You're right. I am so sorry."

"It's nothing. We've been through a lot today."

Mildred nodded but only stood there, staring down at Phoebe while she slept. She looked over at the detective. "If she was possessed, will she remember any of this?"

The man shrugged. "Who knows? Some do. Some don't."

"What do I do about Phoebe?"

He watched her for a few seconds and then cleared his throat. "I will help you carry her to your room. Just tell everyone that she won't be going to dinner because she is not feeling well and is sleeping in your room so you can watch over her."

"What are you going to do?" She wrinkled her nose and rubbed the back of her right hand with the palm of the other. "Can you do something with that spirit board?"

Lionel nodded. "I need to go through her stuff and get rid of anything that has that foul stench on it."

"That would be good. It has caused too much trouble."

The detective smiled and waited while she walked to the other side of the bed. Together they took the sleeping Phoebe down the hall and put her in Mildred's bed.

She looked over at the detective. "Is it over?"

"For now," he said. He met her gaze and took a deep breath. "But it will come back. It will return because the Fallen want nothing more than to make life a literal hell for this world, but it could be generations in the future. Maybe not, though."

"Goodness, I hope it is a very long time."

He reached over and touched the locket around her neck. His hands dropped back to his side. "Be prepared. And ready those coming after you."

Mildred nodded. "I will."

FRIDAY, APRIL 11, 1924

"Burning, burning, burning, burning."
—T.S. Eliot, *"The Waste Land."*

"Why won't you talk to me, Mildred?" Phoebe implored. "We have been best friends for four years. How can you do this to me? After all we've been through?"

Mildred rolled her eyes and tucked the green counterpane back under her pillow. She had ignored Phoebe's moaning and pleading all morning, but grew angrier by the minute. She could feel the heat rising up from her chest. For the past week, she had come to realize how mean and shallow the girl truly was. The fact that she had been possessed only magnified how dark her heart really was to begin with.

Ignoring the pounding on her door, she stood up from the bed and looked around to find something to take her mind off Phoebe's incessant whining and pleading. How had she ever let herself get caught up with such a detestable, malicious person?

Her brush and powder still lay atop the vanity against the back wall. Something else that needed to be straightened up. The thought of Mary falling from the tower haunted her all night to the point she did not sleep more than an hour or two. The poor girl's face, wide-mouthed in surprise just moments before she twisted her eyes nearly shut in panic and screamed. The sound still echoed in her ears. If she hadn't locked Phoebe out in the hall after breakfast where she pounded like some trapped animal, she would have heard Mary's screams over and over.

With a huff, she pulled the vanity chair out and plopped into the seat. The grip of her brush felt cold, tingling in her grip. She looked into the mirror but couldn't even make out her own reflection for the tears that blurred her vision. The brush bit into her tangled hair, pulling sharply at the roots as she angrily yanked the bristles through them. Phoebe pounded three sharp raps on the door.

"Are you going to hold me accountable for an accident?" Phoebe asked. "I wasn't myself. You even said so."

Jerking her head around, Mildred narrowed her eyes and glared at the door. She pushed the chair back, stomping over to the door and jerking it wide open. The smile on Phoebe's face wilted, and she stepped back, holding her right hand to her chest.

"You pushed her, Phoebe." Mildred felt the heat creeping up the back of her neck. "She would have fallen then if J.W. hadn't caught her locket."

Phoebe shook her head. "I didn't mean for her to go over, Mildred. She tripped or something. It's all faded as if I wasn't really there."

Mildred jabbed her finger at Phoebe's chest. "Don't you dare try to lay the responsibility on Mary. You were there. I was there. You even said you could arrange for her to die."

Tears welled up in Phoebe's eyes. "I was only trying to scare her. I didn't want her to think she was as good as the rest of us. She tried to ruin my reputation, my life."

"You ruined your own life, Phoebe. You didn't need any help doing that to yourself. This is all just going to become an excuse about how you couldn't help it." Mildred poked her finger against Phoebe's breast bone, and the thump carried down the empty hall. "You're the one that asked J.W. to take advantage of her crush on him way before you even tried the spirit board."

"But it wasn't love." Phoebe frowned, putting her hands on the sides of Mildred's arms.

Shaking her head and smiling sadly, Mildred narrowed her eyes and lowered her head. "It was to Mary, Phoebe. It was to her."

Mildred winced as Phoebe's fingers dug into her arms. She tried to pull free, but Phoebe gripped her tighter and her lips drew into a flat line. "You're not going to tell anyone, are you, Mildred? I would hate to think that I couldn't trust you."

"No." Mildred jerked her arms free. She took a step back into her room, holding the door in her left hand in case she had to close it suddenly. "You've already trapped me in this web. To tell the truth now would make me as much of a party to her murder as you."

"It was an accident." Phoebe stood in the hall with her arms held out to either side and her palms up.

Mildred scowled. "I don't know what has gotten into you lately, Phoebe. But you are not the person I once thought you were."

Phoebe shrugged. "Just forget about it." She turned and started walking down the hall toward the stairs.

"Hey, Phoebe." Mildred stepped out into the hall and put her hand in her pocket.

"What?" Phoebe stopped and turned back. She looked back at Mildred, her face twisted with disgust.

Mildred smiled and pulled out Mary's locket. "Knowing you and once calling you friend is a stain on my heart that I will carry with me to my grave."

She clasped the chain around her neck, taking her time and making sure Phoebe watched her every movement. The way Phoebe's nostrils flared and the muscles along her jaw twitched as she clenched her mouth sent a quick shiver through her body, but Mildred swallowed her fear and stood up, throwing her shoulders back.

Phoebe lifted her hand and pointed at her. "Don't make me forget that you are my friend. My friends know how to treat me."

Mildred sneered. "I will never forget."

She walked back into her room and slammed the door. Leaning back against it, she exhaled loudly and closed her eyes. The surface of the door suddenly felt cold, and she thought she could feel a little tremor vibrating through its surface. She reached over and slid the lock closed before walking back over to the vanity.

The room felt chilled, but when she looked in the mirror and touched the locket where it rested against her skin, a warmth spread through her chest. Outside her window, she watched as large, white clouds floated over the hillside across the valley, blown by a wind she couldn't see or feel.

Lionel sat in the college lobby, studying the painting *Hounds on the Heath* by Victorian painter Claude Elliston where it hung on the wall against the college president's office.

He studied the elongated shapes of the hounds and their rounded edges but pointed snouts, thinking that he had never before seen a dog that looked anything resembling the animals depicted in the painting. The painting hung in a frame that looked too heavy to hang as casually as it did and would have been taller than he if he took it down off the wall. He couldn't imagine how these painters—or the sculptors during the Renaissance—had imagined such things so much larger than the life they represented.

Several students hurried past, books and papers clutched to their chests as their dresses swished back and forth with each step. Tall windows stretching nearly from the floor to the ceiling fifteen feet above framed the door that led to the back garden, covered by vibrant red velvet curtains. Two of the younger students peered around the edges where the fabric came away from the wall, watching something outside with engaged interest. Every few seconds they would flip pages in the books they held, trying to look like they were studying. Lionel shook his head and tightened his lips.

Why did they always think they were fooling the adults? He knew the activity buzzing through the garden had attracted their curiosity, and they were probably even noticing one of the laborers lifting the paving stones or pushing one of the heavily-laden wheelbarrows. The younger of the two girls caught Lionel's gaze and quickly started tugging on her companion's sleeve. She leaned over and whispered something in her ear. They both kept their eyes down but glanced out the sides at him as they hurried away.

He watched them go and wondered if the youth would ever learn to focus on what truly made a difference in their lives. The thoughts they had, the desires they ached for, and their behaviors indicated most truly the direction and meaning their lives would take. They wasted their time on emotional pursuits like love and passion, when all those things fell into place whether you wanted them or not later in life.

They all needed to prepare. None of them were ready for what lay before them.

"Ah, Detective Peterson." Mr. Thompson's gruff voice snapped his attention away from his own internal ramblings.

He smiled broadly, turning to extend his hand and grasp the other man's. "Good morning, Mr. Thompson. I see that your staff has wasted no time in trying to get things back to normal."

The school president looked over at the garden door and back at the detective quickly, nodding. "Yes. The board thought it best if we got things back to as normal as possible as quickly as possible."

Lionel shrugged. "You're probably right. But does it help to hide what truly happened behind a veneer of new paving stones and fresh flowers?"

The other man frowned, his eyes darting to the garden door and back to the detective. He cleared his throat and pushed his shirt collar back so he could scratch at his shoulder. "What would you have us do, detective?"

"I don't know, Mr. Thompson."

He stepped over to the back door and looked out on the garden. Two workers plunged their shovels into a pile of soil and spread it around the base of a freshly planted magnolia tree. The stones where beautiful young Mary Bencini had fallen to her death had already been removed.

In their place, the school had already set square stones in a grid around a gray pillar. He estimated that all indication anything tragic had occurred in the garden would be removed by the end of the day and business would attempt to go on as usual.

"I just don't think hiding the tragedy from everyone is the best way to deal with it."

The college president squared himself to Lionel. "Then I will repeat my question, Detective. What would you have us do? Do you think it would be best if we kept the blood stains on the path? Or the ones in the hall?"

Detective Peterson sniffed and grimaced. "No. That could be too traumatic."

"Then what we are doing is best?"

"Maybe. I just think we shouldn't try to forget that Mary went to school here or that two people lost their lives in a tragedy that could have been prevented." He took out a handkerchief and wiped away the sweat that beaded across his brow. "But whatever happens, I think that they will be remembered long after anyone else here today. We won't be able to sweep them away."

"And that's not what we're trying to do." Thompson fidgeted, rolling his shoulders and stepping from one foot to the other.

"I know," Lionel reassured him. "I know. I just feel we are already trying to push her memories from our minds, and we shouldn't do that."

"I agree." Thompson nodded. "And the school board will discuss starting an award to benefit similar disadvantaged students in the future."

"Disadvantaged?" The detective felt the sweat rolling back on his forehead.

The older man swallowed, his Adam's apple bobbing in his neck. He took a step back and frowned. "You saw her father. They could not easily afford attending such an institution as this without assistance."

"Disadvantaged?" Lionel repeated. "Was her tuition not paid completely by Senator Mitchell of Kansas?"

Thompson looked at something behind the detective, his eyes flitting back and forth. He started to respond but tripped over his words and had to take a deep breath. "Yes, yes. I believe so, Detective."

Neither of them said anything for a few seconds. The college president shifted his weight back and forth between one leg and the other, while the detective lowered his eyebrows and pushed his tongue against the inside of his cheek. He had obviously made the man question his decisions, and Lionel thought that was a good result. As good as could be considering the tragedy.

Mr. Thompson shook his head and blinked before looking at Lionel. "My secretary told me you had an explanation as to why there was damage to the college and a trail of blood through the halls. The institution has a reputation to keep up."

"Yes, sir," he said. "I had been tracking a suspected murderer, and the trail led to the school."

"Why didn't you get hold of me or one of my staff? We might have been better help than the priest." The college president shook his head. "Poor man. He always worried about all of our students, even the ones that didn't belong to his congregation."

Lionel sucked his teeth with his tongue. "Yes, sir. When I asked Father McHolden for the names of students who couldn't be accounted for at the memorial service, he and I both went to investigate. You had already left and, quite frankly, we didn't have time to look for you."

"Fine," Thompson said, huffing. "Do you know what happened?"

He scowled. "I believe so. Phoebe's window had been broken, and she had been tied up for some sort of ritual."

Thompson nodded. "Then what?"

"We fought the suspect, but Father McHolden was stabbed. The suspect escaped when Mildred Thorton came to check on Phoebe."

"How did she handle that?"

The detective shrugged. "Okay, I guess. She treated the priest's wounds, but he died after I returned."

"Do you know where the suspect went?"

"I am sorry, Mr. Thompson." Lionel shook his head back and forth slowly. "But I could not catch the murderer. He disappeared like ash blown on the wind."

The school president took a deep breath and walked over to the office window. Without turning back to Lionel, he asked, "What kind of beast would do something like this?"

"The worst kind, Mr. Thompson," the detective answered. "The very worst."

He heard muffled voices through the open office door, but Lionel assumed they were people asking the secretary if the president was busy. While Thompson continued to stare out the window, ignoring the voices in the hall, Lionel renewed his study of the painting, still trying to discern whether the topic of the work was supposed to represent greyhounds. They were sort of pointed in the nose, but the animals in the painting more resembled elongated and emaciated horses.

The worst kind.

—

Eureka Springs Chamber of Commerce member George Whitfield owned a drinking establishment tucked away under the Flat-Iron building on Center Street. The small bar had seven open-backed stools against the back wall, while several round tables lay scattered around the room. A billiards table—a new addition, one of which George was extremely proud—nearly filled the smaller, adjoining room to the right of the bar, leaving just enough room for a couple of small tables against the outside wall. Several of the support posts had oil lamps burning in them, filling the room with their warm light. George preferred the dimmer light provided by the lamps, because the electric lights were too bright and would attract unwanted attention.

He had opened the bar just over two years back and kept it low key. Which was all Chief Gaines asked of him, and George was happy to oblige the lawman. Twice in the past six months, he had to go head-to-head with the Eureka Springs Enhancement Society and convince them that he served only homemade, alcohol-free beverages and some local soft cider. Both times, Mayor Fuller had helped him out—Dorothy was a member of the Enhancement Society but Claude was one of his best customers, showing up every Thursday evening like clockwork.

Around three in the afternoon, J.W. Floyd came in and ordered a bottle of George's special black label whiskey. George expected to maybe see the Davidson twins or James Dozier come trailing in after him, but when J.W. removed the lid and lifted the bottle to his lips, he figured Phoebe and the young man had just finished another argument. George shook his head, wondering why a local boy would put up with such a spoiled, hateful woman. She behaved as if she wanted to be away from here about as much as most locals wished her to be gone.

By the time the Davidson twins came in at six-thirty looking for him, the first bottle stood more than half empty on the bar beside J.W. When they tried to get him to go night fishing with them, he lashed out at the air and screamed for them to leave him alone. Shrugging, Frank and Thomas went into the other room and started a game of billiards, leaving J.W. to drown whatever sorrows he needed to forget.

Frank and Thomas both leaned over the billiards table, while the electric, keyless organ whined out a tune from the back corner. They played for the next two hours, asking J.W.—who would only growl—every half hour or so if he was all right or if he wanted to join them. The bar was more than half full now, with several locals watching the Davidson twins and a few patrons from the neighboring towns sitting at the different tables. George could sense trouble brewing and hoped it would avoid his little bar. Something had happened, and no one had told him anything about it. He had started to stack several glasses in the cabinet against the wall behind the bar when he heard the door open.

George looked up to see an elderly man wearing a gray suit come through the entrance, the coat looking rumpled as if he had worn it too long while sitting. He thought the man looked familiar but just couldn't place him right away. Several people turned to watch the man as he stopped in the middle of the room and looked around. His narrow brown eyes squinted as he peered into the billiards room, seemingly studying Frank and Thomas for a little while before moving to someone else. He didn't appear interested in the establishment itself, only in the customers. And that worried George. The last thing he needed—actually he kept a long list of things he didn't really need—was for someone to be keeping tabs on who came and went. Many people came and went through his doors that wanted to keep their extracurricular activities beneath public scrutiny.

After searching the entire place, the man's eyes came to rest on J.W. as the young man sat with his head buried in his arm. He started toward the bar. No one spoke or made a sound, only watched the man. Suddenly George remembered where he had seen him before: Monday night in Kansas City at the Southern Basketball Championship. The man had hugged Mary Bencini after she had run across the court to him, and George realized that the man must be her father. What had happened up at the college the other night had been a tragedy, but how he could avoid any trouble concerned George more.

His eyes met Bencini's, and he could tell that the man was hurting. His shoulders sagged, and each step shuffled more than striking heel to toe as he walked to the bar. He must have felt like he had lost everything. George had heard from Chief Gaines earlier in the day that the man was a widower these past nineteen years. To lose an only child was not something that George ever wanted to experience—he had only one son, his George Jr. The pain had to be unbearable.

Bencini sat on the stool beside J.W. and looked at George. "Do you have any gin?" he asked.

George responded, "Sure. It's not the best."

The man shrugged and put a dollar on the bar. After filling the shot glass to its rim, George pushed the dollar coin back across to the man.

"First one's on the house."

"Obliged." The man nodded and reached out for the glass. As he brought it to his mouth, his lips moved as if he muttered a prayer or something.

Beside him, J.W. stirred, lifting his head from the crook of his arm. "What's with the sudden hospitality, George? You never gave me my first drink free. Hell, you probably charged me double." His words were slurred and soft-edged.

"Mind your own business, J.W."

Bencini threw the gin down in a single toss. He grimaced for a little while, tapping his chest with the side of his fist. He looked over at J.W. and sighed deeply, setting the glass back on the bar.

"Did you intend to wed Mary?"

The question surprised George as much as it did J.W. He looked back and forth between the two men, trying to understand what was happening. After his eyes widened briefly, J.W. reached out and grabbed his nearly empty bottle of whiskey. Turning his head, he glared at the man, his eyes now half-closed.

"Why don't you mind *your* own business, old man," he said slowly and took another long drink from the bottle.

Bencini lifted one eyebrow and slowly shook his head back and forth. "Most people would tend to agree with me that Mary being my dead wife's and my only daughter makes it my business."

J.W. choked and started coughing, spitting his whiskey out all over the bar. He twisted on his stool and looked at the man.

The old man glanced over at George. "Wouldn't you agree?" George just held his hands up, and then started wiping down the bar top with his rag.

"Listen," J.W. said. "My parents would not have let us marry. I am already engaged to Phoebe Stuart, and my father is really looking forward to getting into the oil business anyway."

Bencini nodded slowly. "So you dishonored two women along with their family reputation in that one act."

It was not a question, and J.W. straightened his back. He pushed the whiskey bottle back and rested his elbows on the bar, rubbing his fingertips through his hair while grimacing. "If you only knew Phoebe and her liberated way of thinking, you wouldn't say that." He snorted a short laugh. "It was even her idea."

George watched the exchange. His stomach churned with nervousness, and he noticed someone had switched the organ off. The twins were leaning against either side of the door frame to the billiards room watching their friend's back and forth with Bencini. George looked around and saw every eye riveted to the conversation at the bar. He had seen this before. Grief and alcohol never mixed well and the results were never the ones intended. Carefully, he began putting the lids back on all the drinks and storing them in the cabinet under the bar.

"Then you have brought shame to yourself as well as to my daughter." Bencini pushed his empty glass toward George and nodded at him.

"You're not listening." J.W. kept his head in his hands, his words mumbled. "My parents would not have allowed me to marry a poor girl. They have bigger plans for me."

Bencini nodded as if he understood the dreams parents would have for their child. He blinked a couple of times, his gaze never leaving J.W. "Did you father her baby?"

Every single person in the room must have gasped, but George didn't hear over his own sudden intake of breath. He felt his heart lurch. It wasn't unheard of. But a child being born out of wedlock was something that happened in bigger places than Eureka. Nothing like that ever happened here. The strain would be too much for the Victorian sensibilities of the town leaders to handle. Then George realized that even his wife hadn't known. She and Dorothy Fuller—a woman that had her finger on every pulse of gossip in the town—shared a long friendship going back to high school. He usually knew everything that was going on in the town soon after it happened, but this was new information.

"Yeah." J.W. nodded slowly. "I guess I did."

"Then you should have married her," Bencini said.

"You're still not hearing me." J.W. raised his head. George could tell he was getting angry when his eyes narrowed and he started speaking through clenched teeth. "My parents wouldn't allow it. I would have been cut off."

"Your obligation was to my daughter the moment you fathered a child with her," the older man said. "It would have been the Christian thing to do."

J.W. rocked back on his stool and laughed, pounding his fist on the bar hard enough to rattle the bottles George had stored away beneath it. "What would you Catholics know of Christianity? You're all pagans."

Bencini looked at the young man. When he spoke, his voice reached across the room and remained even. "Obviously more than some crybaby Mama's boy who lets his parents and a woman rule him. Obviously more than a man who thinks more with the shriveled, useless organ between his legs than the one God gifted him with between his shoulders."

George watched the rage build in J.W. The young man shook with fury, clenching his fists until the knuckles whitened. Suddenly, he lashed out with his arm, sending the whiskey bottle sailing down the bar in front of Bencini. It stopped at the end, balancing behind the lip on the edge briefly before toppling to the ground and shattering. Amber liquid splashed across the floor, darkening the wood floors.

"Listen, you fucking wop!" J.W.'s face reddened from the neck up, veins in his neck popping out and his lips turning blue as he screamed. "There was nothing I could do!"

"You could have been a man," Bencini said quietly.

J.W. stood, flinging the stool back with his foot. He turned to face the older man and swung at him, but the man ducked the roundhouse and climbed patiently off his stool. Coming back with his other arm, J.W. again hit nothing but air as Bencini proved to be surprisingly quick for his age and stepped aside.

Bencini backed away as J.W. continued to swing wildly, his arms flailing at the air. His mouth opened as he shrieked, his eyes closed into narrow slits. George looked up at the door when three people near the front left in a hurry. The two men, J.W. lunging and Bencini dodging each strike, moved deeper into the bar toward the back support post. The customers around the tables in the back quickly moved away. The older man retreated until his back rested up against the pole. He didn't try to get around it, and J.W. stopped swinging long enough to see that Bencini couldn't move any further.

His eyes narrowed, and a thin smile split his lips. He lowered his shoulders and charged Bencini. But the older man stumbled to the side, and J.W. barreled into the post. The lamp hanging on the nail above him rocked back, then tumbled down, crashing on his head. The glass reservoir shattered, spilling oil all over his face and down his back—George had filled the oil lamps only an hour earlier.

The burning wick seemed to hover in the air for a moment before settling on top of J.W.'s oil-soaked head. Blue, slow-moving flame spread across his face, moving slowly like sap from a maple tree. J.W. held his hands up in front of him and closed his fingers into fists. The young man's entire body flared up at once, the fire burning brightly, going from the soft blue to a blinding yellow in a flash.

J.W. screamed in terror and ran for the bar. He reached for George, but his burning arm touched the spilled whiskey, igniting a line of fire that raced down the bar and onto the floor.

"Get the water buckets!" George shouted, but the patrons were more worried about escaping as J.W. reeled out of control. He lurched into one table, tipping it up on one side. The glasses of whiskey and gin toppled over, their contents igniting the moment they found flame.

George jumped over the bar and helped Bencini to his feet. He dragged the older man behind him and headed for the door. Bencini pulled free just as they reached the exit and looked back at the bar swallowed up by the fire. J.W.'s body, engulfed in flames, lay motionless in the middle of the front room.

"You could have been a man," George heard the old man whisper.

George looked at the room beyond and watched fire walk along the ceiling like a blue and orange ghost. Several of the tables and the back support pole were already burning. His bar, its mahogany finish bathed in flame, burned before his eyes. People filled the streets with shouts and screams.

He grabbed Bencini around the shoulders and led the man away from the flames. Many of the local shop owners had started a bucket brigade, but George knew it would not be enough. The fire had already broken through the ceiling, and the Spring Street level of the Flat-Iron Building had started to burn as well.

Bencini and George walked down the street into the park around the Basin Spring. Even though they were a hundred yards from the fire, George could still feel the heat against his face when they turned to watch. The flames erupted from the roof of the building, dancing and reaching up into the sky. He looked up when they heard someone shout and felt Bencini's arm twitch. Detective Peterson ran up and stopped by the two men. He leaned over and put his left hand on George's shoulder. He took a few deep breaths before standing up and looking back and forth between the two men.

"What happened?" he asked George.

But Bencini answered before he even opened his mouth. "He attacked me."

Peterson's eyes narrowed and he glanced briefly at the old man before looking at George. Nodding, George watched a piece of ash float by on the wind, swirling back and forth above them in the park before being carried up over the bluff by the wind.

"It was J.W." His eyes hurt, and he blinked repeatedly to try to moisten them as he talked. "He just blew up and started swinging. He knocked over a lamp and started the fire."

He twisted around and stared at the burning building behind them. Flames burned on every floor now, and the heat shattered several of the windows, feeding the fire with more air. Beside him, he heard Peterson mutter something and turned to the detective.

"What'd you say?"

Peterson shook his head and scratched at the back of his left hand with his fingers on the other. "I just said that this is going to get out of control." The detective pursed his lips and exhaled loudly. George glanced up at the man's eyes, large enough that the flames bursting through the roof reflected from them.

"Sure is," George agreed. "It's been a good two years."

Behind them, Bencini shuffled his feet and hung his head. "For you." George barely heard the man's murmur above the din caused by the scurrying on the street and leaned in closer in case he said anything else.

But he remained silent and pushed his hands deep into his suit pockets. A wide smear of black soot streaked the gray material along the side of his right arm. Together the two men watched Bencini walk down the cobblestoned street toward city hall. His shoulders sagged, and his feet shambled along the street. A water wagon and several volunteer fire fighters ran up past him, heading to the fire, the bell clanging loudly.

Just as he passed the Allred Hotel, a red-haired young woman ran up the street, slowing as she passed Bencini. Her eyes darted over at him. She reached out toward him but pulled her hand back suddenly to her chest. Her lips parted as if she tried to say something but shook her head quickly, snapping her mouth closed.

She turned and dashed up the hill. The older man did not even spare Phoebe a sideways glance. He kept walking with his head hung over and watching the street in front of him.

By the time Bencini reached the intersection of Spring and Main Streets, Phoebe had neared the two men. Peterson reached out and grabbed her arm as she flew by them. She fought him, twisting free of the man's grip. When she pulled away, she stepped into the path of a volunteer firefighter rushing to the fire. She toppled over backwards and sat unceremoniously on her back-side in the middle of the street.

George and Peterson darted over to her, grabbing her on either side and helping her to her feet. The detective brushed some rubble and ash off her arm.

"Thank you." She muttered the words and again tried to head up to the fire.

"You can't, Miss Stuart," George said. "It's too dangerous."

She spun around to him, her eyes creased. "J.W.'s in there!" she screamed. Her hands flew to the side of her head. "He goes every Friday."

Peterson put his arm around her shoulders, lowering his voice. "He's gone, Miss Stuart."

She held on to the detective, gripping his jacket lapels tightly in her hands. Her green eyes stared up at him. They widened until George saw the flames in them, moving and twisting like some otherworldly dance.

"Where is he?" Phoebe's hands trembled on the detective's chest. She looked over her shoulder at the blaze. "Is he helping fight it?"

Peterson shook his head slowly and answered her softly, "I'm sorry, Miss Stuart. But Mr. Floyd perished in the flames."

Her hands shook and her mouth opened in a wordless scream. She clenched her hands into tiny fists, and, pounding on the detective's chest, started to wail. Her cry drowned out the roaring of the flames and caused George to wince.

"I love him!" She sobbed. "I wanted to tell him I love him!"

The detective held her against his chest and let her cry, rubbing his hand over the back of her head. "I know."

Phoebe looked up at him, tears streaking through ash and grime on her face in thin, meandering trails. "He will never know, Mr. Peterson. He will never know that I love him."

The young woman crumbled to the street. George shook his head, ash already creating a haze that he squinted to see through. When he looked at the detective and tilted his head to one side, the man only shook his and reached down to Phoebe. Between George and the detective, they pulled her over to the park and set her down on one of the benches. A Studebaker ambulance roared by with its siren screaming, and for a moment, Phoebe and the ambulance screamed together. People ran around the park, searching for friends or family members. George heard one woman cry out for her children and turned to see her grab all three of them, hugging them to her, and then herd them down toward city hall.

He looked up at the blaze, his hand resting on Phoebe's quivering shoulder. It had rained a little earlier in the day but not enough, and despite the overcast sky, it didn't look like it would start again anytime soon. Wind picked up out of the east and blew the smoke and burning debris toward the park. The ash and fire forced Peterson and George to move with Phoebe down to the other side of the spring.

Shaking his head, George found it hard to believe that his fortune had just literally gone up in smoke. The fire burned so intensely it lit the underside of the clouds, and if he couldn't see the flames shooting out of the building, he could have imagined that some false sun had risen in the east to lighten the evening sky. He felt the heat as they walked down Spring Street, thick and heavy on the back of his neck. For the first time since J.W. flung the bottle down the bar, he realized he had been sweating after he wiped the back of his free hand across his brow and it came away glistening and black from the ash.

He knew Peterson had been right, and that the fire was going to be very bad for the town. Phoebe whimpered under his hand as they led her down the hill to city hall, her shoulders still shaking with sobs.

More like a disaster.

―

Carmine sat beside Mary's casket in the back of a T-Model Ford pickup as it pulled out of the hospital parking lot. Harry Mishler—the owner of the *Yellow 37* cab company—gave him the use of the truck and its driver at no charge to get him to the station at Seligman. Even though he had failed Mary and had sent her away to get an education among people that never accepted her, he knew that some people here in this town held good hearts hidden away in their chests. Mary had touched them like only she could. And they had touched her. Each and every one of her letters had told him all the good she found in the people around her. She never once wrote to tell him how she hated being there at the school, or how this person or that had been cruel to her. But he knew they had. He felt it when he met J.W. Floyd, the emptiness in him.

The vehicle shuddered before it began to pick up speed as it pulled onto the road. Something sharp bit into his back next to his spine, and he shifted his weight, never taking his hand off Mary's casket. He looked behind at the hospital.

Elise stood alone in front of the building, watching the truck. Carmine smiled sadly and lifted his hand in farewell. The housemother waved back and lowered her hand to her side as the truck rounded the corner and took her out of his sight. He smiled and watched the shadows from the trees lining the road drift past. "I am glad Miss Elise was here for you, Mary. I'm sorry that I sent you away."

He swallowed and worried at the skin between his eyebrows with his fingers. "But I'm glad you knew her. She is a good woman. And I think she loved you as much as you loved her."

The fire downtown lit the cloud covered sky above it in an eerie orange glow. It reminded him of the arena lights when he had seen Mary at the beginning of the week. Her smile had filled him with such joy. She had been away from their house for nearly a full year now, and as the fire burned several buildings downtown, he was taking her home. He turned away from the town, staring over the cab at the road in front of him. A tear dropped from his chin and splashed against his arm, but he just let the wind blow in his face. He never looked back at the town.

WEDNESDAY—THURSDAY
NOVEMBER 12—13, 2003

"In the faint moonlight, the grass is singing / Over the tumbled graves, about the chapel / There is the empty chapel, only the wind's home."
—T.S. Eliot, *"The Waste Land."*

Shari sat and stared at the older man across from her, ignoring the tear that slipped over her cheeks and dropped to the table. She had never asked her great-grandmother the origin of the locket. She had always assumed Granny Millie had taken the necklace as a childish prank and just felt too burdened by the guilt at the end. When people thought they were getting ready to pass, they usually tried to make amends for past wrongs committed or hurts inflicted. But if what the old man told her was true, then she had been involved in something even larger than even she had suspected.

Or had she known all along?

During one visit back when she was in fifth or sixth grade, she and her great-grandmother had been going through her jewelry box. Granny Millie told her the story of each necklace, ring, and bauble—no matter how trivial—and told her which of her descendants would get which piece. When Shari found that the top drawer had a false back, she pulled it open, but her great-grandmother gasped and slapped it shut before Shari could see what secret it held.

"Not yet, child." Her eyes had blinked several times, and the wrinkles at the edges had seemed to deepen. "One day I will tell you what I need done with that. But it's not time for it to go back. Not yet."

Granny Millie revealed the locket a couple years later. She never told her its history, only that it needed to go back to Eureka.

After shaking her head to clear her mind of the memories, Shari glanced at the man. "Was that all true? How do you know any of that happened?"

The man shrugged. "I'm a little bit of a history buff."

"I haven't seen very much written about the Crescent or its history." Shari picked up her glass and took a sip of chardonnay, letting the wine linger briefly on her tongue before she swallowed.

"But you haven't lived here all your life." He reached into his jacket pocket and pulled out a pack of Lucky Strike cigarettes. He glanced over at the bartender who had her back to them as she put glasses up on the glass shelves against the back wall. He shook one cigarette free and put it in his mouth. "Do you mind if I smoke?"

Shari shook her head. "It's a bar, people do it. Just blow the smoke away from me, if you please."

"Thank you." He smiled, his lips crooked as he held the cigarette between them. "They have a city ordinance against smoking in public places." He shrugged. "But I'm old."

She watched him as he struck his lighter. The end of the cigarette caught quickly in the flame, and he took a long draw. His face lit up from the bright cherry glow as he sucked in the smoke.

After exhaling loudly, Shari took a drink of her chardonnay and set the glass on the table after swallowing. "So what happened after the fire?"

He blew some smoke out over his head, and then looked back at the table. "Well, the Great Dust Bowl hit pretty soon after the fire." He paused and looked over behind her over her shoulder. "You remember all those trees you drove up through?"

Nodding, she brushed at a piece of lint on the table with the back of her fingers. "Yes. It was a beautiful drive."

"Well, those are relatively young trees as far as forests go." He took another draw from his cigarette and exhaled before continuing. "In the late 20s and early 30s, this whole region had been harvested nearly naked, and that bankrupted the Western Lumber Company. John William Floyd, Sr. committed suicide in 1932."

Shari gasped, knitting her brows and holding her hand against her chest. "That's terrible."

The man flicked ashes into his cupped hand, bobbing his head. "Phoebe Stuart ended up marrying three different men that all beat her. She died from alcohol poisoning in New Orleans in 1936. She had been celebrating her thirty-fourth birthday."

Closing his eyes and holding them shut, he breathed in deeply and let it out slowly before he continued. "She never had any children and never accomplished any of her dreams to be involved in the fight for women's equal rights. Her family's oil wells had all dried up by 1927, and the family was implicated in some political blow up or other during the Great Depression.

"The Crescent College and Conservatory for Young Women suffered from the scandal and closed its doors that summer, citing financial reasons." He took another long pull from his cigarette. "That's what President Thompson told the board anyway."

Shari held her glass up to the bartender, asking for more wine, and waited for the man to continue. He licked his lips and held the cigarette in front of him.

"They actually reopened in the fall of 1930 but had to close for the final time in 1933 because of the Depression." He cocked his head to the side and stared into her eyes. "I met your great-grandmother a couple times when she would come back for a visit. But she never told me what she had done with her life. And I never asked because that would have been rude."

Smiling, Shari shifted and pushed herself back in her seat. "Perhaps I can clear some of that up."

"Please do." He leaned forward and put his elbows on the table.

"My great-grandmother moved to Tulsa and married Charles Wheatley, who owned three small grocery stores, two years later," Shari reported. "They had five children—three girls and two boys, including my grandfather."

The old man raised back up and pursed his lips. He nodded, a tight grin stretching across his lips. "So her relationship with James Dozier didn't turn into anything?"

Shari pouted her lips and shook her head back and forth. "Not that she ever told me. And she told me a lot that I sometimes wish she hadn't. Granny Millie may have seemed like a prude, but she had a cantankerous streak in her at times." She lifted her eyes to the ceiling. "Especially after Grandpa Charles passed."

He didn't offer to say anything about it, and Shari continued. "The story you just told me is very similar to the one Granny Millie told me just before she died. She didn't tell me everything and never explained why."

The bartender came over to the table, and Shari waited while she filled her wine glass. "She died when I was twelve and left this to me." She reached into her blouse and pulled out the quarter-moon locket, now a little tarnished with age. It hung from a sturdy new chain and reflected ruddy orange light onto the walls.

The man looked at the pendant and grunted. He didn't ask to hold it or examine it, so Shari tucked it back into her shirt.

"Is that what you came here to do?" He watched her, his eyes seeming to study every line on her face.

Shari shrugged. "I don't know what to do. I know it didn't belong to her, but she had it for sixty years."

The man arched an eyebrow. "She did ask you to return it, didn't she?"

"She never said exactly what to return," Shari responded. "But the locket seems like the only thing she could have been talking about. It is what was in that false back of her jewelry box. She just said it needed to pass to the next guardian. Whatever that means."

The man scratched his right eyebrow and put the cigarette out in his glass of water. He looked around the room, waiting while the bartender took a tray of dirty glasses through the double doors in the back.

"This town is not what it seems." He laced his fingers together and rested his chin on top of them.

Shari grimaced. "What do you mean?"

He leaned back and spread his arms out. "Our peaceful little hamlet hides so many secrets in its dark and recessed corners."

"Like what?" Share transferred her weight to her left hip and stared at the man. The pleasant conversation had suddenly changed directions and become something more ominous.

"We're sitting on the cusp of a gate between two worlds here."

Shari chuckled and sat back. "I know it has its fair share of unusual characters."

The man sat without saying a word for what seemed like minutes to Shari, but which could have only been seconds. She swallowed and licked her lips that had suddenly gone dry. Reaching for her glass of wine, she found it empty and didn't remember that she had drained it.

He shrugged and coughed once. "A lot of people just blow it off as Eureka's eccentricity."

"But it's not?" Shari raised her eyebrows and swung her head to one side.

"Nope." He exhaled loudly, vibrating his lips as the air passed between them. "Detective Peterson knew this."

Shari squinted at the man. Sudden confusion caused her to close her eyes and rub the palms of her hands over her face. She set her hands in her lap. "I don't understand. How do you know what happened in 1924 in such detail?"

"I met Detective Peterson," he explained. He clapped his hands together. "He had been retired for a number of years when I started my service. He told me. He warned me of the battle being waged."

"Battle?"

He nodded. "Between this world and the other. When Phoebe used the talking board, she called something over that wasn't meant to be here. Something that had been cast out."

"A fallen angel?"

"Sure." The man shrugged. "A demon. A phantom. Call it whatever you want."

Shari laughed. "You mean to tell me that all those Sunday School stories were real? They're not just analogies or metaphors to scare children and simple-minded people onto the straight and narrow?"

"A bit cynical, I see?" He reached over and picked his hat up off the table. Rising, he nodded at her and set the hat on his head. "Take care of yourself, Shari Wheatley." He nodded toward her. "Keep that locket next to you tonight. It just may protect you."

Shari watched him turn and walk slowly to the door. The bartender came back in from the kitchen with an empty tray, and the old man nodded at her. He reached in his pocket and wadded something up in his hand. It crinkled like wrapping paper, and he tossed it into the tall gray trashcan beside the bar. With his hand on the door knob, he smiled back at Shari, and then let himself out into the hall. She just sat there in the chair, expecting him to return with an impish grin and tell her that it had all been a joke.

But the door remained closed. The bartender set the rack behind the bar.

Shari watched the woman as she picked up a rag and some Windex. As she walked out from behind the bar, Shari saw her glance down into the trash. The woman gasped and ran to the entrance. She jerked the door open and stood in the hall, looking first to the left then to the right.

Shari frowned when the woman came back. "What was that about?"

Shaking her head, the woman reached into the trash can and pulled something out. She walked toward the glass doors leading out to the balcony but stopped beside Shari's table and looked at her.

"What did you think of one of our ghosts?"

Her heart pounded in her chest, and she had to force herself to remain calm by taking a couple of deep breaths. "I don't believe in ghosts."

The bartender shrugged. "I used to not either when I first took this job two years ago. But I have seen so many unusual things that I started to believe. Tonight really cinched the whole thing for me."

"Tonight?" She raised one eyebrow. "You saw one tonight?"

The woman set the glass cleaner, rag, and the old man's wadded up cigarette pack on the table and then went back into a little storage closet behind the bar. She brought out an old newspaper clipping and set it on the table in front of Shari. It was an article on the Crescent Hotel from the *St. Louis Post Dispatch*.

Eureka Springs—*Legend says four distinct ghosts are regularly spotted in the Crescent. They are: Michael, a redhaired Scandinavian carpenter killed in a fall during the construction of the hotel, crashing through Room 218; a nurse pushing a gurney who is only seen after 11 p.m.—when they carted the deceased out of the cancer hospital; an older gentleman in a top hat who appears at the foot of the staircase on the main floor; and a female student who either fell or was pushed off a balcony and appears screaming as she falls backward out of a window or off a balcony.*

"So you think this was the same old man?" she asked.

"Don't you?"

Pushing the article back across the table, Shari turned to look at the other woman. "But he was wearing a derby and a plain suit, not a top hat."

The bartender scooped the article up and shrugged. "It depends on what day it is. Most times, he is. But he's a bit more casual on Wednesdays."

"What's special about Wednesdays?"

"Who knows?" She stepped to the balcony door, swinging her arm and scooping up the cleaner and rag from the table.

Shari called after her. "I thought you've never seen a ghost. How do you know so much about him all of a sudden?"

The woman stopped with her hand on the brass door handle. She tilted her head up toward the ceiling and exhaled through her nose. "Honey, I've always wanted to believe in them. There isn't a book about the Crescent ghosts I haven't read. I just never had the pleasure of seeing one before tonight."

She pulled the door open but just stood on the threshold, one hand carrying the rag and window cleaner and the other on the handle. A cool breeze came off the balcony, ruffling the woman's hair and stirring the table clothes where they hung over the tables, nearly touching the floor.

"I guess tonight just reaffirmed what I've wanted to believe for a long time." She pivoted around and looked at her.

Shari shook her head, still refusing to believe she had seen one ghost or any other kind of otherworldly apparition. Eureka Springs certainly had its fair share of eccentricity. "But he sat right there talking to me."

"I know." The woman barked a quick laugh that caused Shari's shoulder to tighten. "Usually when people address him, he just disappears."

"This is really all unbelievable," Shari said.

The bartender bit her bottom lip and nodded at the table where the two had been sitting. Shari looked down and saw her empty wine glass and the man's water.

"So?" She knew the woman wanted her to see something, but she could not figure out the mystery.

"You mean to tell me that you've been sitting there for two hours talking to this man and not once noticed that he never touched his water?" The bartender grinned and shook her head.

"Maybe he wasn't thirsty." Shari couldn't think of any other reason why the man had neglected to take even a tiny sip of water.

"Okay," the woman said. But by the way she puckered her lips when she said it, Shari suspected she was humoring her. "But don't you think that after two hours, the ice cubes would have melted?"

Shari walked over to the table and touched the side of the glass. Her fingers felt the bite of the cold, almost numbing, and she noticed also that very little moisture had condensed on the outside of it. The napkin beneath the glass had easily soaked up what had dripped down the side.

"And did you notice the cigarettes he was smoking?" she asked Shari.

"Yes. They were rather strong." She nodded, holding her teeth together and grinning, embarrassed. "I should have asked him not to smoke. I'm sorry."

The woman stuck out her bottom lip. "No problem." The bartender shook her head. "But I'm not talking about their smell. I'm talking about the package."

"What about it?"

"Lucky Strikes." The woman nodded at the package on the table. "Old ones."

Shari shrugged. "I don't understand. They still make that brand."

"Sure." She turned both hands palm up. "But the only place you'll be able to find that dark green package is a museum. Or maybe on Ebay."

Reaching out, Shari grabbed the backs of one of the chairs and pulled it out. Her knees trembled and the room started to spin. Tingling sensations crept up her arm, standing her hair on end. She suddenly found it hard to breathe, struggling for air. Her heart pounded a strong rhythm in her chest like a bass drum. Her muscles felt poised with energy as if she wanted to bolt from the room, but her feet wouldn't move. She pushed her tongue out between her lips, trying to moisten the increasingly strong sensation that she had shoved several cotton balls into her mouth.

"Water." She gasped and struggled to dump herself into the chair.

The bartender hurried over to the bar and opened a bottle of water, and handed it to Shari when she returned. She rubbed Shari's shoulders with the butt of her palm. After taking a couple of swallows, Shari felt like she could breathe again and started pulling deep breaths through her nose.

"Are you all right?" the woman leaned around and asked. She moved to another chair and stared at Shari, her eyes searching her face.

Shari nodded and set the water on the table in front of her. "Yeah, thanks. I think I just need to get some sleep. It's been a weird day."

"It certainly has at that, honey." She picked up the bottle and tossed it into a waste basket behind the bar. "Exciting too, if you ask me."

Shaking her head and blowing out a rush of air through her lips, Shari left the bar and walked down to the north penthouse. As she put her key into the lock, she wondered if she would be able to sleep knowing what had happened almost eighty years ago right above her head. She exhaled and started climbing the stairs.

After brushing her teeth and making sure she had everything packed and ready for the next day, she climbed into the bed and turned on the television set. To feel a little more at ease, she switched the bedside lamp on and pushed the pillows up behind her head. It wasn't long before she nodded off, missing the tail end of *Larry King Live*.

The television must have had a timer because she awoke to a room so black it took her a while to make out the edges of the drapes where light from outside came in through the windows. She knew something had pulled her from a deep slumber filled with dreams of driving a convertible BMW Z3 around the curves and hills of Arkansas Highway 23. The wind had been whipping through her hair, and each turn revealed something straight out of a postcard.

She fluffed the pillow and rolled to her left side, putting her back to the nearly-invisible window and trying to get back to sleep in hopes of recapturing the dream. But just as she started to drift off, she heard her name. Throwing back the covers, she sat up and pushed her back up against the wall. It hadn't come from in the room but had sounded like it had been underwater or through a wall.

"Shari."

She heard it louder this time, more insistent. Still muffled but more forceful.

Reaching over, she pushed the button on the bedside lamp. The bulb flashed, and she heard the pop indicating that it had blown. Her heart raced, pounding behind her chest. She had seen a figure standing at the foot of her bed during the brief moment the light flared up, illuminating the entire room.

Fumbling for her cell phone, she finally grabbed it and tabbed open the flashlight. She shone the light around the room, especially playing it in the corners. Nothing. She put her feet on the floor and pushed herself out of the bed, making her way to the bathroom. A quick search of it and the closet revealed nothing. Looking back to the bed, her heart began to quicken again. Her face flushed and her wrists started to sweat.

Sucking in a deep breath, she swallowed and walked over to the foot of the bed. She dropped to her knees and bent over to look under it, but a wooden frame blocked the space behind the bed skirt.

"Shari." She jumped up and looked down the stairs. "Shari."

She took her sweats off the back of the vanity chair and pulled them over her feet. A quick struggle with an SMU sweatshirt didn't last long, and she was dressed. After slipping on her Adidas running shoes, she crept down the stairs and looked through the security peephole.

The man whom she had spent the evening listening to while he told stories about her Granny Millie stood out in the hall. Kenneth held a silver sword in one hand and a cocked and ready crossbow in the other. When she first looked out through the hole, he had been staring down the hall. But as soon as she saw it was him, he turned back and looked straight at the hole.

"Shari," he said. "We have something to finish."

She swallowed, her stomach feeling like it would whenever she took a zinc vitamin on an empty stomach, like she was sick and couldn't figure out why. Her heart still pounded in her chest, hard enough that she was certain that was how the old man knew she had been looking through the peephole.

"I don't believe in ghosts or demons. Now let me go back to sleep before I call security."

"I have faith your great-grandmother wanted you to help her finish something." He held up the sword. "Now is that time."

Gasping, all kinds of half-formed and chaotic thoughts rushed through her mind. What did he mean now is the time? The time for what? Surely she could reach the phone at the top of the stairs before the old man busted through the door.

"I warned you, mister." Shari whirled around and sprinted up the stairs.

She had only made it halfway up the stairs when she heard the door open behind her. Stumbling, she slipped and racked her shins against the steps. The sudden, intense pain brought tears to her eyes. Through blurry and distorted vision, she saw the old man walking up the stairs.

He stopped on the step below her feet. She thought about kicking him in the face but didn't think it would do anything other than piss him off if he just casually walked through a deadbolt-secured door.

Exhaling through his nose, he shook his head. "I don't have time for this rudeness. We have work to do."

Shari tried to swallow, but all her saliva had dried up. "What work?"

The old man narrowed his eyes. "Were you even listening tonight?"

She nodded vigorously. "Yes."

"Are you wearing the locket?"

Pulling the crescent out from her sweatshirt, she nodded. "Right here."

He nodded once, and then turned back down the stairs. "Then let's go. We have some hunting to do."

The old man led her down the west wing to the window through which she had looked when she first checked into her room. He pulled the long lace curtains aside and opened the window. Before stepping out onto the iron staircase he turned and handed her the crossbow.

"Wait a minute," she said as her fingers gripped the weapon. "How do you know about any of this? What aren't you telling me? I thought you were just a history buff."

Kenneth sighed, letting the air escape his lungs in a great huff. He slowly turned and lowered his eyes until his gaze had captured hers. She couldn't figure out why she was unable to look away. The lights in the corridor reflected off his eyes, as if she was looking through a telescope into the depths of the universe, littered with stars and galaxies that swirled in strange dances, blinking on and off.

"Each time your great-grandmother returned, it was because she had been called." The old detective swallowed. His voice, deep and calm, never seemed to rise in volume, but she never had a problem hearing him.

"She came back to help keep things from crossing over that gate."

"Granny Millie?" Shari couldn't imagine her timid little, great-grandmother doing much beside giving her son-in-laws a hard time or sitting in her chair and telling stories.

"Yes, ma'am." Kenneth nodded. "I think she wanted you to have the locket so you could fill her shoes and fight these battles."

"But I was never called." She tried to make air quotes but couldn't because of the crossbow.

"Why did you come to Eureka Springs today?"

She shrugged. "I've been planning to come visit for years but never got around to it."

"But you did today?" He arched one eyebrow.

Confusion threatened to drown her. Her heartbeat picked up, slamming against her chest. She saw gray streaks crawling across her vision. Taking a deep, even breath, she slowed her heart down enough to answer the man.

"It just felt like the right time."

Kenneth ducked his head under the window and stepped out onto the landing. He bent down and looked back in at Shari.

"You can handle this, can't you?"

Could she? She didn't know for certain. But her Granny Millie had wanted her to bring the locket back. Was it to finish the task? If her great-grandmother believed in her, she must have seen something about her. She took a deep breath in through her nose, letting it swell her chest as the air filled her lungs. Her heart stopped racing and began to beat strong like it did when she went on long runs. Yes. She could do this. Her Granny Millie believed in her enough to give her the task, and she wasn't about to let the spirit of her ancestor down.

Shari chuckled. "Do you have any idea how many times I went hunting with my grandfather?"

"Good." The old man nodded.

She crawled out the window and the moment she stood up, she heard a shriek tear through the night. It caused her to shiver uncontrollably and made her want to flee in any direction. She reached up to touch the locket, and then put it under her sweatshirt so it wouldn't get caught on anything. The first time she heard a fox cry in the night, she had beat her older brother back to the house from the barn. This was completely different. Nothing should have ever been able to make that soul-wrenching noise. It sounded like metal tearing or a chorus of those same foxes on helium.

"Sounds like we got here just in time." He motioned up the ladder. "You go first, if you don't mind."

"What?" Shari protested. "I'm fine with male machismo right now."

He smiled and chuckled. "You have the locket."

"Ah." Shari took a deep breath and started climbing the steps to the tower. She didn't know how she felt about this. Her great-grandmother had done the same thing almost a hundred years ago and some poor girl had lost her life. Today, she was the only woman climbing the stairs.

They made it to the tower balcony without hearing the awful shriek again. But the air felt thick and damp, heavy like a blanket that wanted to smother them.

Shari had never had allergies before, but from her best friend's description, this thickness must be what allergy sufferers felt like all the time. How horrible.

The air grew suddenly colder. Shari heard a scratching noise behind her and whirled around, watching two clawed appendages grab the top of the rail. An elongated body like a greyhound on steroids flipped over the bar and sat on its haunches on the balcony floor.

Lifting the sword above his head, the old man ran at the creature, screaming. But the beast slid around him and charged straight at Shari. She backpedaled until her back struck up against the railing. The thing kept coming. It reached out to slash her across the face but its claws could not get anywhere near her without rebounding as if striking steel. The creature opened its huge mouth filled with multiple rows of needle-like teeth and hissed.

It retreated across the balcony, but Shari jerked the crossbow up and fired from the hip. The quarrel dug into its chest and started to smoke. The creature shrieked in both pain and anger. Its claws dug at the bolt stuck in its flesh. When it turned to leap back over the railing, Shari ran across the platform and tackled the creature to the ground. It thrashed in her grasp, struggling to get free. Its skin started to smoke and blister as she watched.

"Don't let it get away," the old man shouted.

He walked over casually and with one clean stroke separated the creature's head from its body. The severed skull arced across the platform, but the only thing that landed was the little bit of ash that hadn't blown away on the breeze. Shari looked down at the body beneath her and saw nothing but a pile of white powder.

She laughed. "That wasn't so bad."

"Yeah. The easiest it's been in over two hundred years."

"Two..."

She couldn't believe what she had just heard.

"Yep."

"Damn, we're good."

Chuckling, the old man looked at Shari. His gaze grew suddenly serious as he stared at her. "It won't always be like this." He scratched the thin beard covering his chin. "We were successful this time, but the battle will never end."

"Ever?" Shari asked.

"Never. There will be a new cycle with new players in the future. Only

I hope that future generations show the same fortitude that you and your great-grandmother own."

Shari nodded, suddenly somber. How many times did they do this? Would she be called for it again?

"Did Granny Millie ever come back?" She held the crossbow up, and he took it after putting the sword in its scabbard across his back.

The old man smiled. "She was incredible with this crossbow."

Smiling, Shari bobbed her head up and down. "We Wheatley women got this."

"Well, Miss Wheatley," the old man said. "I hope that we do not need to meet again. But you never know."

She watched him climb over the railing and start back down the stairs. Shari followed, but by the time she reached the edge of the roof, the man was nowhere to be seen. Glancing behind her and to the side, she could not tell if he had already slid down the stairs or had simply faded into the night. Shrugging, she climbed down the stairs, crawled back into the window, and returned to her room. The bed felt even more comfortable than it had just before his voice had awakened her. She didn't even have time to think about the events on the platform before she had slipped into a deep sleep.

Shari slept peacefully that night, not waking up until ten the next morning. She showered and dressed, leaving the room after making one last sweep to check if she had left anything. The third floor hall was empty, and she peered through the glass door of Dr. Baker's Lounge as she passed it. A different bartender looked up from behind the bar and smiled, nodding at her while he took glasses from a basket on the counter and set them in the racks above the bar.

The door slid opened as soon as she pushed the call button to the elevator. She stepped over the threshold and pushed the tiny round button with the one. While the lift descended, she read the flyers on the wall again, thinking that a good massage would have done worlds to relax her worn muscles. But she needed to get back to Dallas and wanted to stop in Tulsa to spend the weekend with her parents.

When she stepped out of the elevator, the whine of an electric keyless organ blasted her ears. She eased her way down the hall, stopping to admire a glass unicorn in the gift shop window. Clicking her tongue against her teeth, she decided against it and headed over to the front desk to set her key on the counter.

"How was your stay with us, Miss Wheatley?" the middle-aged blonde clerk asked.

Shari smiled and cocked her head to one side. "I guess you could say it was a bit more exciting than I thought it would be."

"I hope you were able to sleep." The clerk shut the ledger in front of her. "Those ghost hunters can get a little rambunctious. It can be hard on our guests in the middle of the week."

"Oh, yes." Shari grinned, nodding. She hoped the woman found her attitude reassuring. "I didn't even wake up until an hour ago. Very restful."

"Good. We hope you visit us again soon." She pulled a piece of paper off the printer.

Shari bent over and grabbed the handle to her wheeled bag. "Just keep it on the card."

She signed the receipt with her free hand and put her copy in her pocket. She turned to leave. Other than her own Camry and a silver Chrysler 300, the parking lot sat empty. The trunk opened when she hit the button on her keychain. Gravel crunched and popped beneath her suitcase wheels as she walked across the lot. She placed the bag in her car, and after making sure it wouldn't bounce around on the twisting roads, shut the trunk.

Walking around to the driver's side door, she stopped and looked up at the top of the crescent. The late morning sun shone directly down on the roof, driving out all the shadows and mysteries that had been there last night. She saw the ladder and shook her head, amazed at herself that she had climbed those old, metal rungs in the dark.

She got into her car and pulled out onto Prospect, following the old Highway 62 historic loop out of town. Several brightly painted Victorian houses that seemed to have nearly all been converted into bed and breakfasts or restaurants lined both sides of the road. The hospital went by on her left, and she looked back in her mirror.

It must have been the same sight Carmine saw as he headed down this road with Mary's casket in the truck with him.

She sighed and remembered that it had been an overcast, gloomy day when he had left. Today was warm and bright with just enough of a breeze that she rolled her windows down and let the wind blow through her hair. She smiled, hoping that she had completed the task her Granny Millie had set for her all those years ago. Maybe now Eureka Springs could get back to catering to the whims and wishes of the thousands of tourists wandering along its winding streets. Just the way it should be.

Some are born with a silver spoon, but award-winning author JC Crumpton came out of the womb with a pen and a notebook. A cancer survivor, when not writing, reading or working as an analyst, he will often be on the trails or in the gym training for an ultra-marathon or powerlifting—complete with grunts and screams in appropriate places—or volunteering for various charities.

Growing up in a range of places from San Diego, California to Iceland and Germany, JC has a broad palette of experiences to utilize in his writing. He has held a myriad of jobs, including fry cook, telemarketer, soccer coach, substitute teacher, and sales analyst, making him a confused if well-rounded person. He received his undergraduate degree in English with a Creative Writing Emphasis from the University of Arkansas and worked seven years for a daily newspaper, compiling a list of over 1,000 bylines.

Silence in the Garden is JC's first published novel. More of his work has appeared in *Aiofe's Kiss*, *Beyond Centauri*, *The Penwood Review*, and *Saddlebag Dispatches*, among others. He has several projects coming out with Pro Se Press and Oghma Creative Media. He is a proud member of Authors' Anonymous writing group, the Northwest Arkansas Writers' Workshop, Storytellers of America, Ozarks Writers' League, and Ozark Creative Writers.

www.jc-crumpton.com